Mine

LM Kaplin

Broken Brain Books

Paperback ISBN – 979-8-9866751-1-4

First published - August 10th, 2023

Edited by Heather Ann Larson

For anyone who ever loved something
they could never have

MINE

LM Kaplin

Chapter One

CHANDLER HENDRICKS' GRIP ON the knife made him look more like a thug than a chef. He held the handle so tightly his knuckles turned white from the pressure. As he sliced through the onion on the cutting board, he could tell by the awkward position of his arm that his technique made the task harder than it ought to be. Until recently he never needed to learn basic life skills, instead relying on his mother to cook and clean for him. Living together for the past thirty years with no paternal figure in their lives, she had been happy to take care of his needs. Now, with her declining health, all the household chores were thrust upon him with little warning and no preparation.

Chandler looked down at the pile of onions in front of him, his eyes stinging from the wafting aroma. He took a step back and instinctively brought his hand to his face, but rubbing at the corners of his closed eyes only worsened the burning sensation. As he waited for the pain to subside, anger rose up inside him at being forced to perform these menial tasks.

He hated being stuck home all day waiting on his ailing mother. How was he supposed to have a social life when he couldn't leave her side for more than a few minutes? He resented her for his loneliness and placed the blame for it squarely on her shoulders.

In reality, his seclusion from the outside world stemmed from his social anxiety disorder which had been building for much longer than his mother's health problems. Spending half the day as her full-time caregiver—preparing meals, cleaning up after her and administering her medications, only served to multiply his feelings of isolation and animosity.

He thought back to the last time the onions weren't cut to her liking. She threw the tray across the room, shattering the plate and getting tuna fish stuck between the cracks in the floor planks. After doing his best to clean up the mess, the lingering smell persisted two weeks later. The odor didn't bother him much. Being a caretaker, Chandler had quickly become accustomed to off-putting smells.

Stepping back to the cutting board, he placed his hand on the pile of onions to hold them steady. With his other hand, he brought the entire knife up and down recklessly. His motion resembled the use of a hammer rather than a knife. If anyone was watching, they would have been unsurprised when Chandler nicked the ball of his thumb, causing a small flow of blood to leak from the incision. Chandler recoiled in surprise more than pain, dropping the knife and backing away from the cutting board. Bringing his hand to his mouth, he sucked on the wound, causing his glands to salivate at the taste of the metallic-flavored liquid. After a moment, he swallowed the build-up and took a piece of paper towel from the roll on the counter. He ripped it in half and used one piece as a makeshift bandage, holding it in place with his other hand.

Looking at the counter, Chandler noticed a few drops of blood had spilled into the diced onions. Using his other hand, he picked up the tainted onions, annoyed that he would have to start again. Just as he turned to throw them in the garbage, he stopped himself. Instead of throwing them out, he dumped them into the tupperware bowl and mixed the bloody onions with the tuna and mayonnaise. He reasoned that a little bit of blood wouldn't hurt anyone. He was only serving it to his mother. They were family, after all. It's not like he had any diseases.

Hell, he wished he had an STD. At least that would mean he was getting laid. It had been years since he even spoke to a woman, nevermind find one that would fuck him. At least he couldn't catch anything from video clips and camgirls, one of the benefits from getting all his porn online. Besides, Chandler liked to watch—and not just the naked girls on the internet, although he did plenty of that. He liked to people-watch. Strangers at the market or neighbors out for a morning jog. It didn't matter. Even watching them do the same mundane tasks day after day didn't bore him. Any of their lives must be more interesting than his. His favorite people to watch were the residents of his small neighborhood from the safety and security of his home, probably because those were the people he was able to see day in and day out. He had a good view of the street from his position at the counter in the kitchen and from his chair in the living room as well.

He saw Celine Foster across the way, tending her garden. She spent most of the day in the yard whenever the weather was nice, ever since her husband passed away a few years ago. Her two adult children stopped by to visit every week, often with the grandkids in tow.

Celine and Chandler's mother, Rose, had a close friendship. They had been walking partners for many years until Rose could no longer make the trek. After that Celine stopped by to visit often, but as Rose's health worsened so did her attitude. With the increase of snarky comments, Celine came over to visit less and less these days. Chandler would be happy if she stopped coming by altogether. Although he didn't mind watching her from the window, he had no interest in being host to the local gathering of old crones.

Mr. and Mrs. Valentino lived next to Chandler. In their fifties with no children, they spent the winters in Florida, and the rest of the year saw them off on various excursions around the world. They hadn't been home in almost a week, but that didn't stop Chandler from daydreaming about their latest adventure. Chandler knew when they were gone based on the automatic lights that turned on at seven on the dot each night and off again at eleven. Mr. Valentino was a software engineer who sold his startup in the early days of the internet boom and made out like a bandit. He retired early, and now they lived each day like their last, leaving their house empty most of the year while traveling around the globe.

Kevin and Samantha Reed were Chandler's other next-door neighbors. Kevin stood in the front yard throwing a football with their five-year-old son, Dylan. The boy dropped every catch and then threw the ball so wildly his dad usually missed the catch as well. Kevin made no effort to hide his frustration with the young child's lack of athleticism. Dylan seemed more interested in laughing at his dad diving for the ball and falling to the ground than perfecting his aim. Samantha sat on the porch sipping a beverage while she watched her two boys running in the grass. He worked as a police officer while she taught at the middle school in town. They seemed like the perfect family at first glance but living so close, Chandler heard the arguing at night. He knew the sounds he heard from their house were not that of a happy couple. Samantha deserved better than him–so did the boy.

Molly Jacobs lived down the street with her parents. Their house was out of Chandler's line of vision, but she walked the family dog by his house four times a day on a regular schedule – twice in the morning and twice after she got home from school. Molly was one of Chandler's favorite people to watch. The athletically-built teenager would parade down the street often wearing shorts or yoga pants, taunting Chandler with the sway of each step. Having just started eleventh grade, she was entirely too young for Chandler and he would never dream of touching her, but there was no law against looking.

Molly's morning wardrobe consisted of a gray college sweater covering what Chandler could only assume was a pair of tiny shorts. The sweater came down far enough to cover the shorts completely, making her look as if she didn't have pants on at all. Chandler smiled as he replayed the vision in his head. He noticed the sweatshirt said Berkeley College. He wondered if she had applied to schools already. It seemed early considering she still had a semester left of her junior year in high school. Maybe her boyfriend went to school there. He didn't like to think of her having a boyfriend, so he shrugged the thought away. It could be one of her parents' alma maters. He'd check on that later, when he was at the computer.

There were other neighbors, of course, and Chandler knew all of them. Searching online databases and newspaper archives he learned as much as he could about the people he watched from his window. Anything he couldn't find out he fabricated himself. He made up little scenarios for why the couple next door was arguing or what Molly was listening to on her headphones as she walked by with the dog, details of a big arrest Kevin made on the job during a routine traffic stop. Chandler filled in all the tiny nuances of their lives, living vicariously through them in his imagination.

Chandler envied them and he also hated them, too–living their perfect lives, in their perfect homes, with their perfect families. It was so easy for everyone else to go about their business, interacting with other people, holding down a job, and being productive members of society. For Chandler, it took every ounce of courage he had just to order a pizza. And when it came to paying the delivery driver? He might as well have been coming face to face with his father's ghost the way he shook and stammered. The rise of online ordering and contactless delivery was a blessing for Chandler, although these things only served to isolate him from the world even more.

Sure, he had his mother but after living together for thirty-five years, they were both ready for a divorce. But like many married couples, they stayed together out of habit and necessity. He relied on her for money and a roof over his head while she relied on his care. They closely resembled a pair of parasites, needing each other to stay alive while slowly killing the other nonetheless.

Chandler finished assembling the sandwich with lettuce and American cheese, just the way his mother liked it, and placed the plate on her tray next to a small bowl of grapes and a glass of iced tea. Since his mother's last outburst, he began putting a half dose of Xanax in her drink with each meal. He requested the liquid version of the sedative from her doctor after claiming she struggled with the large pills. The doctor barely questioned the request even though she took an array of medicine in capsule form daily for various ailments. By sneaking the Xanax in with each meal, he ensured a few hours of peace as the medication worked its magic.

He picked the tray up by the handles and walked down the hall towards his mother's bedroom.

As he made his way down the hall, the air became noticeably thicker the further he went. The lingering smell of feces and death that accompanied nursing homes and rehabilitation centers hit Chandler's nostrils as he entered his mother's room. He had become immune to many of his mother's smells, but he didn't think he'd ever get used to the smell of a slowly dying human. She might as well have been a living corpse, contaminating the air with her rotting flesh. Being cooped up in this house for so long, he took no notice of how much his body craved fresh air.

His mother lay tilted up on her adjustable bed, the television blaring an afternoon soap opera at almost full volume. Next to the bed lay a rolling table for her meals and a wheelchair. She hadn't been able to get out of bed on her own in months. The only time he bothered helping her up anymore was when she needed to bathe. Even her baths had been cut back to once a week recently.

Chandler set the tray on the table and turned the sound down on the television. The change in volume finally made her take notice of his entrance.

She groaned at the interruption from her show and looked at the tray. Pivoting her gaze back to her son, she said, "I hope this sandwich is better than last time. You know I don't like large chunks of onion. How many times do I have to tell you?"

Chandler thought back to the extra ingredient that made it into his mother's sandwich and grinned. "Yes, Mother. I chopped them twice for you this time. I put my blood, sweat, and tears into this tuna salad."

"I hope you don't mean literally," she replied. "That's not funny."

Chandler laughed. "Of course not, Mother."

She picked up the sandwich and took a bite. Her brow furrowed as she chewed, judging the taste of the meal. Chandler braced himself for the onslaught of insults he knew would be hurled at him any moment.

Instead, to his surprise, she cracked a small smile and said, "Boy, I think this is the best one yet. After all these years, you're finally getting the hang of it. I guess all of my nagging is finally getting through to your little brain."

Chandler bit his tongue and turned around, leaving the room without a reply. It figured she would turn a compliment around to praise herself and end up belittling him again. He was never good enough or smart enough or charming enough for her. And to think he almost felt guilty for putting the bloody onion in her sandwich. It's too bad he'd never get the satisfaction of seeing her find out about it. He imagined her rampage if she ever learned what he had fed her. Chandler would take that secret to the grave.

Chapter Two

CHERRY HILL LANE SAT deserted, as it usually was at this hour in the afternoon. The brisk breeze still carried notes of winter, but the glowing sun indicated warmer weather was on the way. This time of day was always the most boring for Chandler. Most of the neighbors were at work, the kids were still at school, and nothing good was on TV at this hour. Watching the birds chirp in nearby trees or the squirrels fight over acorns wasn't as interesting as watching humans go about their lives.

Chandler got up from his chair by the window and headed to the basement. A few years ago, he spent all his time in the cellar on his computer, only coming up for food, bathroom breaks, or to sleep. His man cave was the only safe space where his mother didn't bother him. With the rise of mobile phones and the decline of his mother's health, he transitioned from his desktop computer in the basement to mobile browsing in the living room. After his mother became confined to her bed, Chandler took over the living room for his use, making it his new home base. From his new spot in the house he could multitask, spending most of the day in his recliner surfing the web and scrolling through memes while watching TV, all with a perfect view out the window.

As he made his way down the stairs, he inhaled and tasted the damp, musty smell of the underground room. The walls were lined with old boxes of miscellaneous items left untouched for decades. Most of the boxes belonged to his father and hadn't been opened since he walked out on them when Chandler was a young boy. His mother held onto the items for her husband's eventual return, but by the time she realized he wasn't coming back, she had become too bitter to do anything with them. Since then, she avoided the basement at all costs, just to keep them out of sight.

One night, Chandler's dad went out to run a few errands, and neither of them ever spoke to him again. Eventually, they received word from his sister a few years later that he died in a drunk driving accident. He was drinking heavily at a bar in Florida and wrapped his car around a telephone pole. Luckily, no one else was injured, but he left behind a new wife and baby. One man, two families, so much heartache.

That's how Chandler found out he had a brother—in the same breath as hearing his absent father passed away. Not that it mattered much, since it was a brother he'd never know. Chandler didn't blame his dad for leaving and starting over. Living with his mom had always been hell, but it only got worse after he left. Now, with her physical decline, she had become almost unbearable. He would leave too, if he could. He imagined himself walking out and starting over, but he wouldn't know the first thing about where to go or what to do. If only life had a reset button, like the old Nintendo collecting dust on the entertainment stand in the corner.

Bare drywall covered most of the walls in the partially finished basement. A few sections of exposed studs were anchored into cement walls. The wall boards were never taped or painted, leaving the room in an unfinished state. Remnant carpeting that fit together like a selection of mismatched pieces from different jigsaw puzzles covered the floor. The thin Berber rug that adorned the section coming off the stairs felt like sandpaper on Chandler's bare feet, but at least it prevented his soles from coming in contact with the cold concrete floor. As Chandler made his way towards his desk, he exhaled in pleasure when his feet came in contact with the luxuriously soft shag carpet surrounding his desk. He loved the feeling of the thick strands brushing between his toes and tickling the arches of his feet.

He sat down in his chair, a black leather office chair on wheels that had seen better days. Most of the seams had come undone, with foam stuffing falling out of every side. Until it collapsed, sending Chandler on his ass, it continued to serve its purpose.

Chandler moved his mouse back and forth rapidly to wake up the computer. The old desktop took longer to resume than he remembered. It was past due for a replacement but with him using it less and less, it was hard to justify another expense he couldn't afford. There was only one thing he still used it for, anyway. Although only a few years ago he played video games for hours on end with this machine, now he preferred wasting his time on the mindless puzzle games that littered the mobile app store on his phone. He doubted this old computer could even run the latest games at this point anyway.

Just like spying on the neighbors outside his window, he liked to watch people online too—mostly girls or couples on the various webcam sites that littered the internet. He would never be able to switch this hobby to his phone. The large, dual-screen monitors allowed him to watch a separate video feed on each screen. Clicking to open a new window and bring up his favorite cam site, Chandler looked to see who was online. He knew most of the regulars names and checked for his favorite. SweetSussie69 was offline, so he scanned the other thumbnails and selected a girl that looked interesting. The well-tanned brunette with her breasts exposed had no bikini lines in sight. She spoke candidly into the camera in the midst of a conversation to her 'fans.' Wearing only a pair of white, high-waist panties, she sat in a chair looking at the camera, talking about her favorite sexual positions in an eastern European accent.

He didn't care for the girls with the robotic fucking machines or fake lips and boobs. Chandler just wanted to watch a normal, down-to-earth girl who looked into the camera and poured her heart out to her viewers. But to Chandler, he wasn't just any anonymous viewer. He felt like the girls were looking and speaking directly to him, as if they were in the same room with each other. Sure, the website had a function for users to tip coins, allowing them to chat with the performers. Some even offered a direct video link where the girls could see him as well, but he knew what they would think after taking one look at him. They might pretend to be interested, but he knew in their head they would be laughing at him the entire time, labeling him a pathetic loser. He was more content watching from the shadows and living out his fantasies in his imagination.

It wasn't even just about the naked girls and his inevitable march toward ejaculation. Chandler felt like he knew each of the women personally. He would be happy sitting there listening to them talk about their grocery list for an hour, and many of them did just that. Sure it was a plus when they blabbered about their day with their tits out, but that wasn't even always necessary. What he really wanted was companionship. Although the girls never saw or heard a peep out of him, he felt like their best friend. More than a best friend. A best friend with benefits.

After Chandler finished his business, he made his way back upstairs to check on his mom and get settled in his spot before activity on the street picked up. By the time he helped her with the bedpan and ensured she swallowed her afternoon medicine, he only had a few minutes before the high school bus came by. He didn't want to risk missing the action, so he ignored his growling stomach and skipped preparing his usual snack, only grabbing a can of iced tea from the refrigerator.

No sooner did he reach the window than the bus rumbled by and came to a stop at the end of the block. With multiple residential developments tightly packed together, a large contingent of high schoolers got off at this stop.

Some kids kept their heads down, going straight for their houses, while others lingered with their friends or avoided their waiting parents. Kristin and her boyfriend Nate always lingered. The couple couldn't keep their hands off each other. Chandler watched them as he held her with their bodies pressed up against each other. His hands cupped around her butt to pull her close. The boy was basically feeling her up in broad daylight. Chandler's anger rose at the blatant public display of affection. He hated them, though he didn't know why. It was probably because they were happy, a feeling Chandler would never know. But as much as he hated them, he wished he was the one making out with her... or someone like her. He'd prefer a girl that didn't let themselves get fondled in the street, but he'd happily enjoy the view that presented itself. Chandler laughed at how pathetic his life had become.

As he watched the teenagers disperse, he wondered what it would be like to be one of them. Their entire future waited ahead, with millions of untapped possibilities. He would kill to be any of them, even the awkward one that reminded him of himself at that age. For Chandler, it was too late, but that kid still has a chance to come out of his shell. You hear about kids going away to college where they make new friends and take on a whole new personality. At thirty-five and still living at home, Chandler never had that opportunity; he never would while his mother controlled his life.

With the kids filtering to their respective houses, it would only be a few minutes before Molly returned with Ash. The medium-sized terrier probably got its name from the color of its coat, but to Chandler, the name always evoked memories of Ash Williams from *The Evil Dead*. He wasn't a huge fan of dogs, but as long as they weren't giant, menacing beasts, Chandler was mostly indifferent to them.

He thought about using the dog as an excuse to talk to Molly, but his anxiety flared just thinking about it, and he couldn't risk the chance of Samantha from next door seeing him chatting with another woman. Chandler didn't want to give her the wrong idea. He had been infatuated with Samantha for years. He was pretty sure she had the same feelings as him, but being married made it hard for her to act on them. Being married to that prick of a cop, Kevin, made it even harder. Either way, Chandler was a patient man. One day, Kevin would be out of the picture and Chandler would have his chance. He knew Samantha and Kevin wouldn't last; he heard them arguing almost every night. She was Chandler's soulmate. Eventually they would end up together, he was sure of it.

While he waited for his love to arrive home, he watched the other neighbors, shifting his line of vision back and forth for anything of interest. Still only 4pm, many hadn't returned home from work yet and the street was empty for the moment. Even Celine Foster across the way had finished her yard work and returned inside her house a few minutes earlier.

Chandler picked up the binoculars from the side table and scanned the windows of her house, looking for any movement. Seeing none, he assumed she was taking a shower after working up a sweat outside. Looking from room to room, it never ceased to amaze him that people left their shades wide open, and not just the senior across the street, but the couple next to her as well. He could see into almost every room of their houses and follow them as they went about their lives. The binoculars gave plenty of detail. The neighboring houses were close enough; there was no need to break out the telescope. The large bedroom windows faced the street, and although the shades were usually closed for any nighttime activities, apparently women of all ages loved prancing around half naked in the morning as they applied lotions, sprays, and an array of other beauty products. He just caught a glimpse here or a peek there as they walked back and forth, but it was enough to allow Chandler's imagination to handle the rest. He bet even old Celine Foster looked pretty good back in her day.

It really was a shame Samantha lived next door instead of across the street, giving Chandler no chance of looking inside her windows. Still, dreaming of living in another house, any other house, and being anyone except for himself would be a step up from his current life. Even the widow across the street had a loving family and a cat for companionship. All Chandler had was his lousy mother.

Chandler glared impatiently at the clock on his phone. Samantha should have been home from picking up her son at daycare fifteen minutes ago. It wasn't like her to be late and he wondered if everything was okay. He considered bringing up the traffic map of her route but thought better of it. It was a short drive, and he doubted that was the reason for their tardiness. As the minutes ticked by, his mood worsened. The precious few seconds watching Samantha go from the car to the house was the highlight of his day. He'd trade all his time in the basement for a few more minutes of watching her.

Chandler watched from his window as the forest green Subaru finally came into view down the street. Pulling into the driveway, Samantha exited the car with a bag of groceries. She stopped at the store. Chandler felt silly for thinking the worst, but knew his fear for her safety just meant that he cared.

Samantha looked as beautiful as ever. She wore a loose-fitting, yellow blouse and jeans with her silky red hair pulled back in a ponytail. He could see Dylan in the backseat. It would take her a few minutes to help him out of the car and bring everything inside.

She put the groceries down on the blacktop and opened the rear door. As she leaned in to unbuckle her son, her shirt hung down enough to expose her undergarment. Instinctively, Chandler picked up the binoculars sitting on the end table near the window and put them to his eyes. Plenty of practice allowed him to zoom in and focus on the correct spot almost immediately. He thought about taking out his phone but knew he'd never be able to open the camera in time, so he resigned to enjoying the view while it lasted.

The binoculars gave him a perfect angle down her shirt and he caught sight of the white cups of her bra. Unfortunately, the bra covered almost the entirety of her breasts and prevented any cleavage from showing, but he knew exactly what they looked like underneath–no imagination necessary. The bra looked expensive, not that he knew what an expensive bra looked like, but the material seemed thick and plush. He wondered if it was as soft as her skin underneath. No. He couldn't picture any material being that soft. He imagined standing behind her with his arms wrapped around her in a loving embrace. Chandler felt a twinge in his pants, but just as quickly as the show started, it ended. Samantha stood up and took a step backwards letting Dylan hop out of the car.

As much as he enjoyed watching Molly walk by in her yoga pants, Samantha was a real woman, and his fantasies ran much deeper with her. She used to be friendly towards Chandler when they first moved in next door, but over the years, she became cagey around him, and ever since Dylan was born, she seemed like she wanted as little interaction with him as possible. Chandler guessed it had to do with her husband. He seemed to be the controlling type, and Chandler wouldn't be surprised if her spouse forbade her from speaking to other men. By Samanatha keeping to herself, her husband had less reason to raise a hand to her.

As much as Chandler hated talking with most people, Samantha was the exception. Living directly next to each other they couldn't help but run into each other occasionally. She was the only woman, basically the only human, that Chandler could be himself in front of without clamming up and putting his awkwardness on display. That's why he timed his trips out of the house when she might be out as well.

Samantha picked up the groceries and fumbled with her keys as she unlocked the front door, entering the house. Dylan remained outside, playing with a toy in the yard. Kids differed from adults. Full of innocence, they saw the best in people. Children didn't judge people the same way adults did, and Chandler felt more comfortable talking to children.

Chandler stood up and put his sneakers on. This would be the perfect time to check the mail. He often planned his trips outside at the least likely opportunity to run into a neighbor, but he used it as a chance to see Samantha and Dylan as often as he could. Running outside as she pulled in would seem a little suspicious, but with her currently in the house he could strike up a conversation with Dylan, maybe make the kid laugh at a joke, and when Samantha came back out, she would see them together having a good time. He didn't know much about moms, but he knew that one way to get on their good side was to be nice to their kid.

Chapter Three

FUMBLING WITH HIS LACES, Chandler missed the loop and had to begin again. The clock in his head counted the precious seconds wasted that could've been spent outside talking to Dylan. He made a mental note to get slip-on shoes at his earliest convenience. By the time he exited the house and made his way down the walkway towards the unattended child, he knew he wouldn't have much time left before Samantha returned. The boy was old enough to stay out of the road, but his mother wouldn't leave him alone for more than a few minutes. Ideally, Chandler would check the mail first and strike up a conversation with the kid on the way back, but he didn't have time for the display so he made a bee-line for the boy. Even if Samantha saw him approach the boy directly through the window, why should it matter? Why shouldn't he say hi to the child? Despite his unease, Chandler breathed a sigh of relief when he reached the boy with no sign of movement from the house.

"Hey Dylan, how's it going?" Chandler said as he neared the child. Dylan looked up from his game but didn't give a reply. "Did you have a good day today at daycare... or school? Whatever you call it."

Hesitantly, the boy nodded his head. Chandler racked his brain for what to say next. He failed to think this far ahead. Kids weren't hard to impress though, right?

"So.. what's your favorite animal?" he asked the boy.

Dylan replied after a few awkward seconds. "I like monkeys. My stuffy is a monkey. See?" he said, holding up a blue stuffed monkey in his hand. The tattered plush toy had been well-loved over the years and seen better days.

"What's his name?" Chandler asked.

"I just call him Monkey," said Dylan.

"Oh. Well, he's got to have another name than that. I don't think you'd like it if everyone just called you Human. Have you ever even asked him?" Chandler said.

"Asked him?" the boy said inquisitively.

"Of course. You speak Monkeneese, right?"

"Monkeneese?" asked the child, confused and curious.

"Yeah, it's the universal language of monkeys, and I just happen to be an expert in it. Virtually all monkeys can speak it fluently. You can usually get your point across to apes, baboons, and gorillas as well."

Dylan looked at Chandler with a blank stare, his mind trying to process what the man said, unsure if he was being serious or joking.

"Come here, let me show you," said Chandler.

Forgetting about his shyness and interested in what Chandler wanted to show him, Dylan crossed the driveway in front of his mother's parked car until they stood within each other's grasp.

Chandler cocked his head as if he were listening to an unheard voice. Tilting it again in the other direction, he curled his hands towards his armpits and moved them up and down in his best impression of a primate, making whooping sounds at the stuffed doll.

Dylan stared wide eyed at Chandler. Even if his neighbor could speak with animals, he was old enough to know that his stuffed monkey couldn't possibly communicate with anyone considering it wasn't real.

After a moment of his ridiculous display, Chandler looked at Dylan and said, "He said his name is Jasper and... hold on a second." After a few more exchanges with the stuffed animal, Chandler shook his head and turned to the boy. "Did you hear that? Your monkey hasn't had anything to eat all day. Get this monkey some ice cream, pronto!"

Dylan broke out laughing at the ridiculous statement and wondered how the man could be so weird, talking to a stuffed animal and offering it ice cream. "It's not a real monkey," came Dylan's reply. "It doesn't actually eat food."

"Real or not, everybody knows monkeys love banana splits."

The child furrowed his brow but smiled. "You're silly," he said. "Do you want to play tag?"

Unsure how to reply, he just said, "Okay."

"You're it!" Dylan said and tapped Chandler on the leg before turning to running away towards the other end of his yard.

Before Chandler knew what he was doing, his legs carried him after the boy, his hand outstretched attempting to touch him. For a few moments, Chandler forgot all about his problems and even about Samantha. He was a kid again, no older than Dylan, laughing and having fun with his friend. The boys had a lot in common, and he was lucky to have a friend his age living next door. It's too bad their mothers wouldn't let them out to play with each other very often, but for these few minutes, they were free to do anything they wanted.

The feeling of the cool air on his face as he ran, chasing his friend, exhilarated Chandler. The rush gave him a boost to run even faster, until he was within reach of the boy. Just as he was about to touch Dylan's shoulder, the child turned his head to look at his pursuer. While looking back, the boy missed a dip in the ground and tripped, sending him tumbling forward.

Chandler, unable to stop in time, crashed into the fallen boy, accidentally kicking him in the abdomen. His balance lost and his legs twisted together, Chandler fell down on top of the child. Worry came over him, hoping the boy was unharmed by the fall. Dylan sat up with a frown on his face, looking directly at Chandler. Sure the boy would break out in hysterics at any moment, Chandler feared the worst. To his surprise, the frown turned into laughter as the boy came away shaken but unscathed.

Hearing the commotion, Samantha came running outside the house. She let the screen door slam loudly as she exited. "Hey! What are you doing? Get off my property! What did you do to him? Dylan are you alright?" The string of commands and questions came hurling at the duo laying on the grass as quick as the woman who shouted them.

With the boy's mother angry and fast approaching, Chandler felt his body tense for the confrontation. His plan for winning over Samantha was back-firing. He should never have crossed onto their side of the property. He could have had a conversation with Dylan from his own side, without the physical interaction, but he lost track of himself and just wanted to have fun. The boy wasn't hurt. He didn't understand why Samantha would be so angry.

"I'm sorry. We were just playing. He's fine," replied Chandler as he backed away from the child.

"Yea, Mom, I'm okay. We were just playing tag," added Dylan.

Samantha turned to Chandler and said, "Listen, I know this is hard for you to hear but please. Just leave us alone."

Almost as if on queue, a squad car pulled up and turned into the driveway, coming to a halt only inches from where Chandler stood.

"What's going on, guys?" the uniformed officer said, looking back and forth between Samantha and Chandler with a look of unease.

"He was just leaving," replied Samantha before adding, "I'm still trying to figure out why he came over in the first place." She knew of her husband's animosity towards their strange neighbor and hoped to avoid blame for Chandler's unwanted visit. Although Kevin provided well for his family, their tensions ran high, and Samantha wanted to prevent setting off his short-fused temper.

"Sorry, I was... uh, just getting the mail and Dylan asked to play tag," Chandler said, still retreating towards his house.

Kevin stared at him with rage burning in his eyes. As Chandler reached the front steps, his neighbor yelled to him, "Stay on your own property and don't bother my family!"

Chandler wanted to tell him the only person bothering his family was him, but he thought better of the retort and quietly went inside the house. He wondered if Kevin would take out his aggression over the incident on his wife.

Chandler was woken on numerous occasions to the sounds of yelling and household items being thrown. Kevin's overt threats of physical violence toward his wife had Chandler imagining himself running next door and barging into their house to save Samantha from her abusive husband. He pictured himself dashing into the house like a superhero to defeat the villain, who in this case wore a police uniform. Sweeping the damsel away to safety, they would fall madly in love and live happily ever after. An infinite number of these scenarios would play over and over in Chandler's mind. In one version, he burst through the door and beat the man to a bloody pulp. In another, he picked the larger man up over his head and hurled him through the bay window in the living room.

Chandler lived within these imaginary storylines, getting lost in his thoughts for hours upon end with no regard for the passing of time or his surroundings. Eventually, he would come back to reality from the sounding of a car horn or his mother's call. Sometimes he got lost in his daydreams for so long the only thing that brought him back to reality was the pressure on his bladder. He had half a mind to just stay in his waking dream and piss himself rather than make the long trip to the toilet, but he knew he'd regret that decision later. Snapping out of his fantasy, he made his way down the hall to relieve himself, the cold tile on his feet and harsh bathroom lights solidifying his return to this realm.

He preferred spending time inside his head rather than facing the reality of his dismal life. If Chandler was born 100 years later, maybe he could have lived inside *The Matrix* or *The Oasis*, only coming out of the VR world when truly necessary, but of course, he wasn't that lucky.

It was easy to see why Chandler preferred living inside his fantasies. In the real world, going next door to save the woman of his dreams would end with him being the one bleeding on the ground. Even if he somehow got the upper hand, Kevin's police buddies would arrive, and it's not hard to guess which side they would take.

Nevermind the fact he couldn't save someone who didn't want to be saved.

It baffled him what she even saw in the overweight policeman. The guy looked dumber than a box of rocks. Every time Chandler spotted him wearing that uniform, it reminded him of *Paul Blart Mall Cop*. That bastard didn't deserve Samantha.

Chapter Four

CHANDLER KNEW VIRTUALLY EVERY car that drove down Cherry Hill Lane. The residential street sat away from the main section of town and didn't get much through traffic. So when two cars he didn't recognize came rolling slowly down the street, his curiosity piqued. Chandler's interest in the visitors only grew when they came to a stop in front of the Reed house.

The occupants of the first vehicle exited the car. The woman carried a tray of deviled eggs. Something was happening at the Reed house. A party? Chandler searched his brain. No holidays approached, and none of the Reed family had birthdays this month. He considered other reasons for them to throw a party. Nothing came to mind. Some people just had parties for the sake of having a party. Chandler cringed at the thought of mingling with so many people. For him, being caught in awkward social situations was a nightmare.

More guests arrived by the minute, lining the street with their cars. Chandler studied each of them as they made their way into the Reed house. He recognized none of the faces but knew every detail of their lives.

He gave them each names and a backstory as they came into view, part of a game he liked to play in his head.

This couple walking to the front door was Mark and Megan Beauchamp. They stopped at the grocery store on the way to pick up a package of cupcakes. Megan had baked a homemade batch but fell asleep at the kitchen table while they burned to a crisp in the oven. She awoke when the smoke detector screamed in alarm throughout the house. Mark ran in from his office after hearing the obnoxious sound and another fight ensued about his wife's excessive drinking.

The next couple, Jordan and Janice Patridge, ran the town's historical society. Jordan also owned and operated a chain of successful hardware stores. As revered members of the local community, they keep their dirty laundry as far from town as possible. That's why they just drove two hours to admit their son in a drug rehab center, chosen because of its remote location and low chance of being recognized during their visits.

Chandler went on making up these intricate descriptions for all the visitors as they arrived. His mind was well trained in the art of inventing these imaginary scenarios. Eventually the guests stopped arriving and Chandler's attention turned. As luck would have it for the Reeds, the sun shone bright overhead without a cloud in the sky. Although still the end of winter, the near perfect weather allowed the gathering to assemble in the backyard. Chandler could already hear the sound of overlapping conversations permeating through the house.

Although he had no view of the Reed's backyard from his normal spot, there was a perfect view of the party from inside his house. He just needed to watch from the window in his mother's room. Chandler was past the point of caring what she thought, so he entered her room and took a position in the corner by the window.

The guests loitered on the neatly manicured back lawn, some standing while others sat in camping chairs arranged throughout the space. A jungle gym with swings and a slide entertained the younger kids while the adults chatted, enjoying beverages and appetizers. A few sipped soft drinks while many drank beers as they awaited the assorted meats Kevin prepared on the grill. Chandler wondered how many of the guests were off-duty police officers.

He slid the window open, first a crack and then a bit more. The close proximity to the neighbor's yard allowed him to listen in on their conversations but his mother's blaring television drowned out the voices.

Rose Hendricks, almost completely engaged in her show, hadn't even noticed her son's entry. That changed as soon as he lowered the volume on the television. Her words came flying at him almost immediately. "Why are you always turning off my show? I don't touch your things," she said.

"Mom, you can't touch my things. You don't even get out of bed," he replied.

"Don't be snarky with me. How quickly you forget all the years I spent raising you. I gave you your privacy down in the basement, even when I knew you were up to no good. Maybe that was the problem. I let you rot your mind on video games and smut. You brought the devil into this home and I allowed it. Now my body is failing me while my mind is still sharp. I guess I'm getting what I deserve for raising such a worthless child."

Chandler wanted to yell at her, scream at her. Instead, he held his tongue and pictured the surprised look on her face of seeing him pick up a spare pillow and smothering her with the cushion. In her weakened state she wouldn't put up much of a fight. A little struggle, sure, but he had no doubt of his ability to end it quickly for her and release them both from this painful existence. Although these thoughts of matricide danced inside his head, he doubted his ability to go through with the act. Instead, he'd remain stuck in the same old rut he's been in for way too long.

Rather than continue the screaming match with his mother, he turned his back on her and looked out the window once more. To his embarrassment, many of the party guests were looking in his direction and whispering amongst themselves. Chandler never considered that if he could hear them, they could hear him as well.

He slunk away from the window, crouching down on the floor below. He wrapped his arms around his legs and huddled into a ball, hoping and praying no one saw him. Chandler imagined their conversations, asking each other about the strange man who lived next door. "He couldn't find a wife, so he fights with his mother all day long." *What makes them any better than him? Riding on their high horses, laughing at poor Chandler. They can keep their judgements to themselves. They don't know him and never would.* He could almost hear their taunts, as if shouting their disparaging thoughts at him.

Chandler stood up and pushed the shades aside, letting the breeze from the open window hit his face. He stuck his head through the opening and shouted at the partygoers.

"Shut the fuck up you pigs! Leave me alone!"

As the words left his mouth, the yard came into view and he realized none of them had been paying him any attention at all. Was it all in his imagination? If they heard the argument with his mother, they had moved on with their conversations.

The outburst instantly muted the entire party. A sea of shocked faces peered back at Chandler. Even the kids playing on the swings skidded their feet, bringing them to a stop while they gawked at the source of the yelling.

Chandler froze. He wore the same shocked expression as everyone else. He wanted to close his eyes and sink out of view, but his muscles failed to obey his command. Frozen in place, he felt paralyzed.

As the guests stared with shocked expressions, Chandler scanned the crowd until his eyes locked with the only face wearing a different expression. Kevin stood by the grill, his face beet red with rage. His complexion looked the same color as the slab of raw meat on the tray next to him. Kevin wasn't going to be insulted in front of his friends. With a look of determination, he put down the tongs and left the crowd, making his way toward his disruptive neighbor.

Chandler moved away from the window, panic setting in. Always acting without thinking first. Now what was he going to do? Kevin would be here any moment. He could ignore him, wait him out. But with so many people next door watching, he couldn't hide away like a wimp.

He'd answer the door, make a quick apology, blame his short temper on the argument with his mother and that would be that. No harm, no foul.

A second later, the pounding on his door began. He heard Kevin yelling from the other side, "Hey! What the hell is wrong with you?... Screaming and cursing at people? Kids even! Open the fuck up and face me like a man."

He considered mentioning the irony of Kevin now also cursing with children in earshot but decided it wouldn't improve the situation. Chandler approached the door slowly, giving his neighbor time to calm down. However, the incessant pounding only increased in intensity. The sound of Kevin's voice grew more furious with each second Chandler delayed the confrontation.

Finally, he turned the deadbolt. Kevin's yelling stopped after hearing the clicking lock. Chandler's offer of apology began as soon as the door opened, begging forgiveness and hoping for a quick end to the awkward encounter.

Before Chandler could finish his sentence, Kevin pushed the door open and entered the house, grabbing the front of Chandler's shirt. The off-duty officer twisted Chandler's shirt and pulled him forward, causing the fabric to tighten around his neck.

In a deep growl, he said, "I don't know how many times I have to tell you to leave us alone. Whatever weird little fantasies you have about my family, my wife... What? You think I didn't know? That's all they are, fantasies, and that's all they'll ever be. Any woman would take one look at you and laugh at the thought of letting you fuck them. You're nothing more than a feckless loser. Nobody likes you on this street. I'm guessing no one liked you your entire life. No wonder your daddy left and your mom hated you for it. Everyone knows you sit around spying on people all day, you creepy son of a bitch. You're the reason I installed security cameras, so Samantha feels a little safer when I'm not home. Now stop bothering my family and my friends. Pervert."

Without waiting for a reply, Kevin released Chandler and turned, marching out of the house and back to his own yard.

Chandler seethed at the intrusion. His clenched teeth felt like they could break in his mouth. The pressure building inside his skull was unbearable. How dare this man come into his house and say those awful things. He had better things to do than spy on their party. He felt like following Kevin outside and pummeling him into the ground. Punching the bastard in the face repeatedly. He saw it vividly in his mind. Even after knocking the man unconscious he would continue to attack him like a rabid animal. Chandler pictured the horror on the party guests' faces while he beat their host senseless. He'd relish snuffing the man's life out in front of his friends.

Reality, of course, would be much less forgiving to Chandler's attempted intervention. He knew his neighbor's solid build and police training would allow him to turn the tables on Chandler in an instant, likely leaving Chandler the one laying on the ground, beaten to a bloody pulp. But in Chandler's distorted vision, he twisted reality and fantasy into his own perfect utopia.

Chapter Five

ONLY SECONDS PASSED SINCE the asshole next door had barged into his house and left just as quickly, but the passing of time was meaningless to Chandler. His ears rang louder with each beat of his heart. Dark spots swam through his vision and he felt the walls closing in on him. The front door stood wide open, just as Kevin left it when he angrily stormed out. Chandler remained frozen in place, staring off into the distance, thinking about the harsh words from his neighbor.

To make matters worse, the grating voice of his mother, yelling from down the hall, snapped him out of his thoughts. "Chandler! Who was that? What was he saying? Chandler! Come here this instant!" Her voice sounded worse than nails on a chalkboard. No matter how bad things got for him, he always had his mother, the one constant that grounded him in this awful reality.

Chandler blinked his eyes rapidly as he broke from his trance. The ringing in his ears morphed into a pounding in his head. Dealing with his mother was the last thing he needed. He didn't owe her an explanation. Why couldn't she just mind her own business?

He closed the front door and called back to her. "Just leave me alone. I have a headache. I need to take a nap."

"Not until you tell me what he was talking about! Plus, I'm due for my medicine. Come here and tell me what he meant about spying on people."

No matter how much he hated her, she trained him well and he couldn't deny her demands. Begrudgingly, Chandler trekked down the hall towards her room, stopping at the bathroom to take something for his headache. He opened the medicine cabinet and grabbed the bottle of Advil. It sat along a row of pill bottles–various medicines the doctors had prescribed for him over the years. Most did nothing to help his mental state, and many had physical side effects ranging from an upset stomach to violent seizures. Needless to say, Chandler stopped taking all of them once his mother could no longer force him to. He dry-swallowed two of the brown, circular pills for his headache and continued down the hall to his mother's room.

Upon his entry, she repeated her demanding questions. "What was that racket about? Was it the officer from next door?"

"Mom, you know what that was about. They heard us arguing, and he came over to ask us to be quiet. They have guests over."

"Not that part, stupid. I know they have guests over. I have ears. Everyone heard what you yelled out the window, for christ's sake. I'm talking about the part where he said you're spying on them and scaring his wife."

Embarrassment overcame Chandler. Sure, his mom had an idea what he was up to but being confined to her bed, she didn't know the extent of his voyeurism. He wished he didn't have to deal with this on top of everything else. Why couldn't she have dementia instead of these physical ailments? Then he wouldn't have to put up with her prying into his life. His ideal scenario would see his mother as an inanimate object in the corner with no mental capacity for demands or interrogation. The only thing he needed her for was her money to pay for the house and food.

He wondered how much longer he would have to deal with this situation. Sooner or later, something had to give. Finally, he replied in as calm a manner as he could muster, "Please, just stay out of my business."

"People bursting into my home is my business too! Have you forgotten whose house this is? If you don't watch yourself, I'll kick you out of here. You think I won't? You need me more than I need you. I could hire any college student to help me around the house. Maybe finally being on your own would be good for you. You need to take some responsibility for your pathetic life. What are you going to do when I'm gone? You'll probably end up out on the street. A loser, just like your father."

Chandler clenched his fists in anger. He wanted to break her nose. She deserved it. As he contemplated punching her, the doorbell rang, breaking the tension. The unexpected sound startled them both. Muttering to himself, he left the room to answer it, "That asshole is back again? I've had it with everyone intruding in my life!"

Chander marched towards the door, furious at the repeated disturbance. He felt the hate inside of him. He had plenty to go around. This time, he wouldn't be so meek. He looked around the living room for some sort of weapon and picked up a brass candlestick. He lifted it above his head and opened the door, his chest puffed out and ready to strike.

"Stay the fuck away from...," he yelled, but froze in shock when he saw Celine Foster standing before him. She wore an equally startled look on her face, petrified of the menacing man before her. She cowered in front of the raised weapon, shrinking down even further from her already meager stature.

"Oh my god, Mrs. Foster. I'm so sorry. I thought you were someone else," blurted Chandler as he lowered the candlestick. "Please. I'm really sorry. I've had a rough week."

The woman took a moment for her nerves to calm before replying. "I can see that. I guess this is a bad time, but I saw what happened earlier with Mr. Reed. I just wanted to stop by and make sure everything was okay."

Chandler's eyes blinked in rapid succession. Unprepared for this encounter when he already had so much rattling his cage, he just stared at her, offering no reply.

To break the awkward silence, she added, "I know your mother and I haven't been as close recently and I'm partially to blame. She's going through a tough time and I should have been more understanding. I can only imagine it must be very frustrating for her. I shouldn't have abandoned her the way I did. Maybe I could visit with her for a minute. I think it would be good for her spirits."

The words barely registered with Chandler. He wanted to slam the door in her face. He didn't care if the force of the door closing knocked her backwards down the front steps and onto the hard walkway. Chandler pictured her laid out on the cement path with a cracked skull and broken ribs. He forced a smile and said, "I'm sorry, but you're right. This is a bad time. We had a slight disagreement, just a little tiff. You know how it can get, stuck at home with the same person for years on end. We're bound to get on each other's nerves a bit. Thank you for checking in on us."

As usual, Chandler took no regard for other people's feelings in the situation. Mrs. Foster, having lost her husband several years ago, didn't know what it was like being stuck at home with a close family member all day. She wished she did.

Chandler saw her expression change at the statement and continued, stumbling over his words as he went. "The issue with Mr. Reed. It's no problem either, just a small misunderstanding. If you come by tomorrow, maybe my mom will be up for a visit. It's just really not a good time."

Mrs. Foster resigned herself to the fact that she wouldn't be getting to see her friend and didn't feel like pressing the matter. Having watched Chandler grow up from a young boy, she knew of his quirks and has seen the progression of his mental illness. Celine knew better than anyone how close he staggered to the edge of sanity. She pitied the boy and empathized with the family's plight, but as he grew older, she recognized his bizarre behavior only grew worse and his outbursts more violent. She worried for them, but she had always been taught to stay out of other family's matters.

"Okay, well, I will stop back again. Please tell her I was here. And I know this isn't easy for you either. If you ever need someone to talk to, I'm always available." Mrs. Foster turned around and stumbled as she went down the three cement steps, losing her balance and almost falling to the ground before catching herself on the railing.

Chandler thought he probably should offer to help, but he shut the door and went to his room for a nap. He ignored his mother's calls as he put in his earplugs and drifted off to sleep.

Chapter Six

THE VERY NEXT DAY, Chandler sat in his chair looking out the window once again. Still stewing over the encounter with his neighbor, he spotted another car he didn't recognize roll down the street. The small, blue hatchback driven by a young brunette pulled right into the Reed's driveway. More house guests so soon? No. It was Monday and the Reeds weren't even home. Probably a solicitor peddling beauty products or magazines, or maybe a religious nut, spreading the word of the Lord.

Unfortunately for her, both Samantha and Kevin were at work this time of day. Chandler hoped she wasn't planning on making her way down the street. He had no interest in whatever she was selling, regardless of how pretty she might be. He harbored no false hopes that the woman would be attracted to him and had no interest in her sales pitch. She sat in the car fiddling with something in her lap, probably her mobile phone. It seemed strange that she parked in their driveway instead of on the road, yet she sat in her car, making no move to exit.

Chandler didn't have to wait long to see the reason for her visit. A minute later, Kevin's police cruiser rolled up and came to a stop in front of the house. He parked on the street and got out of his vehicle. When the woman in the blue car saw Kevin, she opened her door and exited hers as well.

Standing in the driveway, Chandler now had a full view of the woman. She wore a white button-down shirt covered by an open gray blazer with a matching skirt. The skirt stopped just above the knee, with dark nylons covering the rest of her legs. Her outfit was clearly designed to attract attention.

She waited by her car for Kevin to approach, and they embraced as they greeted each other. He whispered something into her ear while they hugged and she laughed. Chandler wished he heard what they said. After parting, Kevin led her up the walkway and unlocked the front door, allowing the woman to enter. He followed her inside, closing the door behind him.

Chandler couldn't believe his eyes. He knew Kevin treated his wife badly, but parading another woman right through the front door during the middle of the day! The man's infidelity was no shock to Chandler, but surely Kevin would have some discretion in his actions.

Nevermind the fact that this woman looked to be in her early twenties; she was at least a decade younger than his neighbor. Why would she be interested in a married, overweight policeman ten years her senior? It made no sense. Chandler marveled at how easy it was for some guys and figured it must be the badge. Women were enamored by the power it brought.

He had half a mind to call Samantha and tell her to come home immediately. There's no better proof than catching a cheating spouse in the act. He pulled out his phone and brought up the dial pad before remembering he didn't even know her number. Undeterred from his quest to expose Kevin's infidelity, he switched over to his camera app. The next best proof would be photo or video evidence. With the pair inside the house, he wouldn't be able to get any shots of them until they exited, but he snapped a few photos of the woman's car in the meantime. Unfortunately, from his angle the license plate sat out of view. He contemplated going outside to see it but cringed at the thought of another confrontation with Kevin. Besides, he needed more proof than a few photos of an empty car in the driveway.

He thought about their home security system. The exterior cameras would show the visit, but that wouldn't be enough, either. If they had any cameras inside the house, those might tell a different story. Either way, he guessed their security footage wasn't something Samantha normally even looked at.

It's been years since Chandler was inside the Reed house - well before the exterior cameras were installed. He didn't know if they even had interior cameras. Those would surely offer the proof Chander needed. Chandler was good with computers but suddenly he wished he was a skilled hacker, able to access any system. Imagine the hours of fun he could have spying on people inside their homes. The gears in his mind spun through the limitless possibilities.

He saw himself bypassing firewalls and decoding security keys, all to peek in on his unassuming neighbors. But why stop there? With unrestricted access to any network in the world, he could be a millionaire... no, a billionaire. Once he possessed a bank account with no limits, Samantha would notice him.

It wouldn't be enough to just win over Samantha. He wanted Kevin to feel his pain. He needed Kevin to feel humiliated and helpless for a change. Hacking his home security system and exposing the details of his rendezvous would be a good start, but with unlimited computer access, the options were endless. He could start by getting him kicked off the force. Maybe an old drunk driving incident would pop up on his record? No, plenty of cops had questionable pasts with prior arrest records swept under the rug. This needed to be something bigger... like a DNA match on a cold case murder investigation. Something Kevin wouldn't be able to talk his way out of. The corners of Chandler's mouth curled upwards in an involuntary smile as he thought of the ways he could ruin his neighbor.

A slamming car door brought Chandler back to reality. A sense of panic came over him immediately. He had been so lost in his imagination he failed to notice them leaving the house. He missed his chance for a photo! How could he have been so careless? Kevin sat in his cruiser looking back at the house. He started the engine and drove off, leaving the woman standing alone in the driveway.

Chandler fumbled with his phone and focused the camera on the woman. Luckily, she hadn't entered her car yet, allowing Chandler to take a rapid succession of pictures. Double checking the screen, he confirmed the picture clearly showed her face. He wondered if Samantha would recognize the woman when she saw the photos. He guessed it would be easier on her if Kevin's mistress was a stranger rather than an acquaintance or a friend. Either way, Chandler would be there to console her. This could be the chance he'd been waiting for.

He considered the best way to break the news to her. Ideally, he would let her down gently, but considering their awkward relationship, he didn't know how that would be possible. Any interaction with her would only last a few seconds, so he had to choose his words carefully.

Chandler kept the camera focused on the woman and her car. He had enough pictures of her but wanted to get a snap of her plate as she drove away. Instead of getting in the driver's seat however, she walked to the rear of her car, popped open the hatchback, and leaned inside.

Her tight skirt showed off her slender curves as she leaned into the trunk. Since Chandler was already in position, he snapped a few pictures of the woman as she bent into the car, reaching for something out of view. The slit on her skirt crept up her legs, exposing the tops of her rear thighs. Pressing the shutter button repeatedly, he considered how lucky Kevin was to have such an amazing wife and this hot piece on the side. If Chandler were lucky enough to be with a girl like Samantha, he would never think of cheating on her, regardless of how tempting the other options were. Still, he was in awe of the ease with which Kevin got laid.

The woman slowly backed away from the car holding something large. She struggled with the awkward size of the item in her arms. When she turned around, Chandler couldn't have been more shocked than if she had been holding a dead body. He couldn't believe his eyes. The woman made her way to the front of the lawn and hammered the sign into the grass. The sign read Silver Acre Realty with the woman's picture and phone number on it. They were going to sell the house. How could this be possible? They couldn't move. How would he keep tabs on them if they didn't live next door? Chandler didn't care if a sorority moved into their house, he couldn't lose sight of Samantha. And having watched the boy grow up all these years, he felt a closeness with him as well. There was only one answer. He would follow them. He could easily find out where they were moving to. There had to be other properties available nearby. Or maybe he could stop them from moving. Yes, that would be better. His financial situation didn't offer him many options for getting a new house. Plus, imagine the red flags when they noticed him hanging around their new neighborhood. He could picture the restraining order now. He would find a way to stop this. He had to.

Chapter Seven

CHANDLER PRESSED THE FINAL number on his phone and put the handset to his ear. He cleared his mind and took a deep breath, attempting to work up his courage while he waited for the phone to ring. A piece of paper with his speech sat on the coffee table in front of him. Even with the prepared notes, he felt a lump rise in his throat before opening his mouth.

Speaking on the telephone had always been awkward for Chandler. Calls with the few friends he'd had over the years were filled with weird interactions and awkward silence. Needless to say, none of his friendships lasted very long. This time, he remained determined to act like a normal person and be more outgoing. He didn't have any time to waste.

After the fourth ring, a female voice picked up and said, "Hello, you've reached Dana Summers at Silver Acre Realty. I'm probably with another client right now, but if you leave your name and number, I'll get back to you as soon as I can."

"Hello, uhhh Miss Summers. My name is Ronald Kelly, and I saw one of your signs on Cherry Hill Lane. I was wondering if I could see the house. The best time for me would be weekday mornings. I want to see it as soon as possible. Please call me back at 719-266-2837. Thank you."

He repeated his script like a robot but breathed a sigh of relief that he didn't have to speak with anyone. All of that preparation had been for nothing and now he had to be ready for the return call. Not knowing when the phone would ring kept his anxiety at an increased level. He wouldn't have time to practice for the conversation, but at least he delivered the message.

Chandler didn't have to wait long for the return call. Five minutes later, while fixing his mother's lunch, his phone vibrated on the laminate countertop. Putting the food aside, he glanced quickly at the caller ID, although he knew who it was. The only calls he received were for offers on how to reduce student loan payments or extend his car warranty, neither of which he even had.

"Hello, Mr. Kelly? This is Dana Summers. You called me a few minutes ago. Sorry, I was on the road. You were interested in taking a look at the house on Cherry Hill?"

"Uhm, yes hello. I've just moved to the area and looking for a place to, you know... for a house."

"Great! I'd love to show you the property. We're planning an open house for this weekend, but I could probably get you a sneak peek before that if you want. Are you available tomorrow morning for a tour?"

"Yeah, I guess that's fine. Are you... you don't.... Is it possible to see it today?"

"Hmmm, well, let me check my schedule real quick. I have a few showings scheduled already."

"Oh, I uh, I understand if you can't," he replied.

"Listen, I know how it is to be excited for a new house and want to get first dibs on it. I can cut one of my meetings short and meet you in a couple hours... say, around eleven o'clock?"

"Yeah, sure, that would be great. I'll.. I'll see you then."

"Great, thanks, bye bye!"

Chandler ended the call, feeling proud of himself. The conversation went as well as he could have hoped. He abandoned his mother's lunch unfinished on the counter and went to his room to change. He couldn't very well meet this woman in an old t-shirt and sweatpants.

Opening his closet, he pushed the clothes aside, allowing him access to the hangers hiding in the far end of the rack. He hadn't worn his dress clothes in years and only had a few outfits that still fit. He selected a pair of black slacks and a blue, button-down shirt. The stale smell of the long untouched clothes tickled his nose as the freshly agitated dust particles filled the air. Hopefully Dana wouldn't notice the musty smell. Maybe a few minutes in the open would help them air out. He planned to go outside early, anyway. It wouldn't do for Dana to see Chandler exit his house and walk next door for the showing.

After putting on his clothes and about ready to head out the door, he heard his mother's call. Glancing back at the clock and then towards the kitchen, he remembered her lunch. In his haste to prepare for the meeting he had completely forgotten about her. Besides being hungry, she was also overdue for her morning meds. On the plus side, he still had over an hour before his appointment with Dana. Still plenty of time to take care of his mother and be ready for the appointment.

"Sorry, Mother, I must have dozed off again. I'm finishing your sandwich now and I'll be right there," he called to her.

"Nevermind the sandwich, come here!" she yelled from down the hall.

Chandler groaned. "Mother, I don't have much time. I'm going out in a few minutes. I need to feed you before I leave." Ignoring her request, he finished preparing the food as quickly as possible and made his way down the hall.

"Where are you going? You never go anywhere," she asked after he set the tray down on the rolling table in her room.

"I'm just going to meet someone for a few minutes. It won't be long."

"Meet someone, hmmm? Are you forgetting I have ears? Ever since you were little, you've always raised your voice when you talk on the phone. I couldn't help but overhear your conversation."

"Mother, please. Mind your own business. I'm old enough to make my own decisions."

Rose burst out in a bout of laughter that turned into a coughing fit. "Have you forgotten what that man said to you? What do you think he will do if he finds out you were inside his house? Your obsession with that woman next door has got to end, and apparently they feel the same way. I think them moving away will be for the best for everyone."

He was sick of her know-it-all attitude and could hold in his temper no longer. Raising his voice, he yelled, "You don't know anything about what's best for me! You never have!"

"Snooping around the house next door... You think that's healthy and normal? You are not normal. I never wanted to admit it, but I always knew there was something wrong with you. Instead of sitting around and brooding about your life all day, why don't you do something productive and clean the bedpan? That's about all you're good for, and lately you haven't even been doing a good job of that. I don't know how I failed so badly with you. You're worthless, just like your father."

That was it, the last straw. Chandler was done putting up with her insults.

He replayed his vision in his head, grabbing the pillow and holding it tight in both hands as he pressed it down over her face. He wondered how long it would take until her life had been snuffed out. Enough imaginary daydreams. No more visions of another life. It was time to take action.

He leaned in close to her. The pillow under her head beckoned him forward. His arms stretched out to reach for the cushion, ready to yank it from under her skull. His body felt rigid; filled with hate and anger but also nervousness of what he was about to do. He felt the emotions swirling inside of him. His arms crept closer to the pillow, but time screeched to a halt. Everything moved in slow motion. As he approached her, a look of confusion came over his mother's face. Then, almost involuntarily, his hands made a last second detour and instead of grabbing the pillow, he found his fingers closing around her throat.

If she had been nicer to him he would have let her go out with a soft cushion, but she deserved to feel the pain that he had felt for so long. She needed to understand what he went through as a young child with no one to teach him how to be a functioning part of society. But the real reason for his altered execution plan were her eyes. He wanted to look into them while he killed her. He wanted to see the fear in the last moments of life as her soul left her body, something he couldn't do with a pillow over her face.

As Chandler tightened his grip around his mother's neck, her hands reached up for him. She scraped her fingernails against his cheek, but he extended his arms, pulling his face back and out of reach. As his hands grew tighter, he felt the muscles in her throat pulsing, trying desperately to open the airway he had sealed off.

A gurgling sound escaped her throat while her eyes bulged open in horror. He felt her struggling under his weight. Her arms flailed at his sides, reaching up for him. She grabbed at his arms, but his shirt prevented her from finding purchase. Her legs kicked wildly on the bed, but they did nothing to improve her situation. Her brain sent signals of panic throughout her body as the organ used up the last of its oxygen.

The frantic struggling only encouraged Chandler to squeeze tighter. He squeezed with all of his strength until he heard an audible crunching sound as her ruined esophagus caved in on itself.

The kicking ceased and everything became still. As Chandler's labored breathing subsided, a quiet came over the room. The deed was done. His mother was dead. Everything would be different from this point on. There was no turning back. His mother was right about one thing. There would be no more sitting around wallowing in self pity. With his metamorphosis underway, it would soon be time to emerge from his cocoon.

Chapter Eight

FREEDOM. NEVER IN HIS life had Chandler Hendricks known the feeling. His mother's corpse lay in the other room, still warm, yet he couldn't wipe the smile from his face. His biggest regret was that he hadn't killed her years ago. Adrenaline coursed through his veins as he paced back and forth in the living room, high from the rush of the kill. He couldn't even tell if his feet were touching the ground. It felt more like floating. His hands ached from the pressure he exerted while strangling his mother, but the sensation just added to his buzz.

He lost track of how many times he replayed the killing in his head, relishing the memory, searing it into his brain. It was a memory he planned to savor, keeping the feeling of the kill with him for the rest of his life. His thoughts focused only on the last seconds of her life and her expression as she expired. His memory loop finally broke when he noticed the blue hatchback rolling down the street.

"Oh shit," he said, shocked free of the memory and suddenly remembering the meeting with the realtor. He looked at the clock; he only had ten minutes until their appointment. Now what would he do? He couldn't let her see him leaving this house. "The back door," he said, still speaking to himself. "I can get into their yard from the back."

He flew out the sliding glass door in the kitchen and down the steps, descending from the small deck to the yard below. The Reeds had installed a privacy fence between the yards but luckily, it didn't stretch around the entire property. Chandler easily snuck around the rear and into their yard just as Dana exited her car.

Chandler emerged from the gate leading from the backyard, surprising the young woman. Instinctively her hand went straight to the canister of pepper spray she always kept in her purse. Having plenty of run-ins with guys who wouldn't take no for an answer, she felt more at ease having the extra line of defense on hand. She pulled it out, ready to spray, but upon seeing her reaction, Chandler raised his hands, showing he meant no harm.

"Hi, I'm sorry to scare you. I'm Ronald. I talked to you on the phone... about looking at the house?"

"Oh. Hi Ronald, you gave me quite the startle. You never know who is prowling around these properties. I'm Dana Summers, Silver Acre Realty," she said, holding out her hand. "Burglars see the For Sale sign out front and think the house is easy pickings. Better safe than sorry, ya know." She dangled the pepper spray in her hand before returning it to her purse with a nervous smile.

“Sorry about that,” he said. “I got here a few minutes early, so I was just looking around back. I guess I should have waited for you.”

“It’s alright. Usually, the owners leave the gate locked,” she replied. “I guess they forgot to close it before they left for work.”

Chandler accepted her hand and tentatively shook it. The firmness of her grip and hearty shake surprised him. As a well-trained saleswoman, Dana had spent hours perfecting her handshake, and her grip seemed like a vise compared to Chandler’s limp wrist. It was something he still needed to work on if he wanted to fit in as a member of society.

“Are you okay? You’re bleeding,” she asked, gesturing to her cheek.

“Oh, this?” he said, wiping the scratch on his face and looking at the red residue on his hand. He had completely forgotten about the injury from his mother. “I scraped it earlier. I thought it had stopped bleeding.”

“It looks pretty deep. You should clean it and get a bandage. Anyway, I didn’t see a car out front,” she said.

“Oh. Yeah, I walked over. I’m staying close by. With a friend. It's not far.”

“Well, that’s convenient. So you’re already familiar with the neighborhood? That must be how you saw the For Sale sign so quickly.”

“Yes,” he said, followed by a prolonged silence. Although proud of his performance so far, he was quickly running out of steam. Unsure what to say next, he hoped for a quick end to the pleasantries.

Dana saw the awkward look on his face and helped move the conversation along. "Follow me and I'll give you the tour. If you have any questions, don't be shy," she said, turning and beckoning him to follow.

The sun reflected off Dana's long, dark brown hair as she walked. Any woman would envy her petite size and perfect features. Chandler knew she was attractive just from seeing her through the window, but up close he could truly behold her beauty. She was one of the prettiest women he had ever encountered. Although his heart belonged to another and he had no genuine interest in Dana, he had no qualms about admiring her assets as he followed her inside.

Although her mace had been tucked safely in her purse, Chandler noted Dana's tense posture as she led the way to the front door. He didn't blame her for being skittish. He imagined his disheveled appearance and bloody face made him look like a lunatic. If that's what she thought, she wouldn't be very far off from the truth.

He entered the main living area, and the first thing Chandler noticed was how orderly everything looked. A pile of neatly stacked magazines was the only occupant of the small wooden end table next to the leather sofa. The carpet looked freshly vacuumed, still having the stroke lines left by the machine. In the corner of the room, methodically arranged inside a clear plastic bin, sat all of Dylan's toys. Chandler figured with a child Dylan's age the room would be in disarray. The possibility that they might have tidied up for the showing never even entered his mind.

Touring the kitchen and the other first-floor rooms, he scanned the ceiling edges for any security cameras. Seeing none, he realized Kevin probably didn't want any evidence of how badly he treated his family.

As he walked from room to room, Chandler pictured himself living in the house. It was a perfectly normal thought for any prospective buyer but in his mind, the current owner's family came with the house. Slipping right into the role of loving father and husband, he'd treat Samantha worlds better than Kevin did.

"Do you know why the family who lives here is moving?" he asked.

As a trained salesperson, Dana was well-versed on what to say and what not to say to prospective buyers. She always put a positive spin on the reason any house was for sale. Her go-to responses usually included something about the owners moving out of state for a new job opportunity or needing to find a bigger house due to a growing family.

Choosing her words carefully, she said, "Well, it's supposed to be a secret since they haven't announced it yet, so don't say anything, but the owners are thinking about another child and they're looking for something with an extra bedroom. You know how it is." A big smile came across her face. Years of practice allowed her to turn on a happy face with the flick of a switch, regardless of her current mood.

No, Chandler didn't know 'how it is.' He'd never had a relationship that progressed past the first few dates. Family planning was never an activity that even entered his radar. The news caught him off-guard. He hadn't considered the possibility that the Reeds might have another child. The timing of the house going up for sale so soon after their fight made it easy for Chandler to link the two activities as being related, but now he questioned everything. In a strange way, he felt proud at having such a profound impact on the couple that they were uprooting their lives and selling their house because of him. Now, after hearing this, he felt small and more insignificant than ever. If Samantha were to have another child, he should be the father.

Chandler's anger rose in his chest. He pictured himself grabbing the real estate agent by her throat and squeezing, crushing her neck and giving her the same fate as his mother. He could easily overpower the smaller woman. His hands balled up into fists as the rage festered inside him.

He took a deep breath in an attempt to calm his anger. He couldn't blame the messenger. To anyone but Chandler this would be joyful news. Dana was clueless about his feelings for Samantha. His mother deserved her fate, but this woman did not. His hands relaxed and his fingers unfurled.

Attempting to force himself to move on from the thought of his love pregnant with another man's baby, he asked, "Arethebedroomsupstairs?" The question came out of Chandler's mouth so quick it sounded like a single word, his way of trying to push his thoughts to a new topic.

"They sure are. There's two bedrooms upstairs. Follow me and we can take a peek."

Chandler tried to suppress a groan. He could find the bedrooms on his own. Most of the houses on the street had similar layouts. The small, two bedroom Cape Cod style home was hardly a maze. Chandler was hoping to take his time while looking around without someone breathing over his shoulder while he snooped.

He followed Dana up, running his finger along the top of the wooden banister as he went. On the wall hung picture frames of the family in various poses over the years. The cherry-picked photos might paint a picture of a perfect family, but Chandler knew the truth about them.

The master bedroom door stood open near the top of the stairs. A king-size bed, covered neatly in a burgundy comforter and sheets, sat in the center of the room. Tall, white bed posts loomed over the room from the corners of the frame. An ornate headboard sat against the far wall. The headboard looked like it came from a princess's room in a child's fairy tale. Chandler never understood the purpose of such extravagance. Beds were for sleeping, in the dark. He pictured himself walking into one of the posts while going to the bathroom in the night. He'd have to talk to Samantha about changing the frame after he settled in.

Two dressers occupied empty spaces along the walls. The long dresser by the foot of the bed was barely visible between the copious amounts of lotions, body sprays and hair accessories sprawled across it. This one clearly belonged to Samantha, while the tall, skinny dresser on the adjacent wall, covered in clothing, deodorant, and other junk, housed Kevin's clothes.

He wanted to look through her drawers, but knew better with Dana in the room. Instead, he headed towards the walk-in closet where Samantha hung most of her outfits. Upon entering the closest, he took a deep breath, hoping to catch a whiff of Samantha's scent but instead, he swallowed a gulp of stale leather and moth balls.

The unpleasant aroma made Chandler question what he was even doing. What was he hoping to achieve by coming here? Was this one last walk through Samantha's life before she moved away, never to be seen again? Or was it a reconnaissance mission to find a way to prevent her from leaving at all? Maybe subconsciously he hoped to find evidence of Kevin's mistreatment of Samantha and use it to weasel his way into her life. Chandler didn't know. He hadn't even thought that far ahead. He just knew that he needed to be close to her, and being inside her home was the best he could manage in the current situation. Doubts ran through his head as he questioned his actions and regretted his decisions, par for the course in Chandler's life. He spent a lot of time dwelling on past actions or conversations and imagining what he could have done differently, but rarely did he use the insight to guide his future endeavors. In almost any public situation, panic set it and he made the same social mistakes over and over. The story of his life.

The ringing in his head returned, filling his skull with a familiar melody. He recognized the tune but couldn't place it. It grew louder and louder until he heard a woman's voice singing along with the music. A pop song. He looked at Dana and realized the song came from her phone. She checked the receiver and then looked at Chandler.

Seeing his opening he said, "Please, don't mind me. I'm almost done up here."

"Okay, I'm sure it will just take a minute and then I'd love to hear what you think of the place. If it isn't for you, just be honest. I have some other properties you could see as well." She turned and headed out of the room, answering the call as she went downstairs.

Alone, he looked towards the dresser and felt an overwhelming urge to rifle through the drawers. Maybe he would take a pair of panties home for safekeeping. However, the problem with the freshly washed garments in the drawers was they would smell more like laundry detergent than Samantha. Instead, his eyes drifted towards the bed and he wondered which side she slept on. The stack of romance novels on the left nightstand gave him the answer. Walking over to her side of the bed, he placed his hand on the pillow, the same pillow where she rested her head every night. He noticed a few strands of her bright auburn hair on the pillowcase.

The next thing he knew, his face was nuzzled against the soft cotton fabric, and he breathed in deeply, finally getting the scent he longed for. He squeezed the pillow tight, imagining it was Samantha he held instead of a plush, inanimate object. Chandler wondered what she wore to sleep at night. He pictured her sleeping in the nude or skimpy lingerie, but he knew she was probably more of a t-shirt and comfy pants kind of girl. He had no problem with that. Reveling in his fantasies and huffing her pheromones, Chandler closed his eyes and drifted in and out of consciousness.

"Excuse me, Mr. Kelly. What are you doing?"

The real estate agent's shrill voice woke Chandler from his nap. He jumped up from his fetal position on the bed. "I... I was just testing out the bed to see if I'd like it. It was so comfortable I lost track of myself."

"The bed doesn't come with the property," she replied with an incredulous look on her face.

"Oh. Right. Yeah, of course. I'm really sorry. Nevermind that," said Chandler. "We... uh, we can go now."

Unsure if she should offer to show him the rest of the home, Dana kept quiet and followed him out of the house. She wanted to end this meeting as quickly as possible. She had been around enough sleazy guys in her day to spot one a mile away. Her guard had been up since the moment they met. Finding him curled up in the owner's bed was beyond bizarre and the icing on the cake. She hoped not to hear from the strange man again, regardless of her commission on the sale.

"Thanks. It was nice to meet you," he said while walking towards the road, planning to take a loop around the block and swing back after the real estate agent left. The street looked empty. He hoped none of the neighbors noticed him coming out of the Reed house. Glancing from window to window, he wondered who else liked to watch from the safety of their houses.

Chapter Nine

THE CONSTANT PATTER OF raindrops hitting the roof echoed in Chandler's ears. The dreary day meant little activity on Cherry Hill Lane for Chandler to observe. Instead, he stared aimlessly out the window at the pools of water in the road and considered the events of the previous day. The ripples from the rain hitting the surface mesmerized him. A car would drive by every few minutes, splashing the puddles as they went, and Chandler stared out the window in a trance, lost in his thoughts as usual.

He couldn't shake the embarrassment of yesterday's meeting with the realtor and pondered to himself how bad the incident had been. On one hand, he realized it must have been strange for her to walk in on him sleeping in the Reed's bed–spooning the pillow no less. On the other hand, he could have just gotten off a long shift at work or have a condition such as narcolepsy. It's not like she caught him with his pants down or rummaging through her undergarments. All things considered, it could have been worse.

The alarm on his phone beeped. Fifteen minutes before noon, it was time to make lunch for his mother. Chandler stood up from his chair and made his way to the kitchen before realizing he hadn't even checked on her all day. Usually she would have called for him by now. After he prepared her usual sandwich and brought it to her, he stopped in his tracks when he walked into the room.

"Mother. You haven't even touched last night's dinner yet. Are you feeling ill?" he asked. The lifeless corpse lying in bed gave no reply so he added, "Mother. You need to wake up and eat something to help with your strength. You're looking very pale today."

He eyed the plate of grilled chicken, rice, and corn and said, "You know, you're right. It's cold by now. Try this instead." He took the old plate, replaced it with the freshly prepared lunch, and closed the door as he exited the room.

On his way to empty the untouched meal in the garbage, the doorbell rang twice followed by a pounding on the front door. With his mind still swimming in his own thoughts, blocking out the horrible act he committed against his own blood, Chandler barely registered his actions as he moved to open the door with the plate still in hand. If he had looked through the peephole before unlocking it and saw the angry police officer standing on his stoop, he might have decided not to answer the door at all.

As soon as he turned the handle, the door burst open–kicked in by the visitor outside. The unexpected burst of energy caught him off-guard and Chandler stepped backwards, losing his balance in the process and landing on his rear. The tray with last night's dinner went flying to the floor, spilling the contents across the carpet.

Kevin stood in the entryway, dressed in his uniform, his eyes blazing with anger and hatred. He received word from the realtor about the strange behavior of the prospective buyer and immediately brought up the surveillance footage from the outdoor security cameras on his phone. Upon seeing Chandler's less than stealthy entry from the backyard, he told his supervisor he had a personal matter to attend to and took the rest of the day off. He drove straight home and marched directly to Chandler's house.

He stepped through the threshold and said, "You're dead, you little bitch. This isn't a fucking game."

Chandler looked up at him with his mouth open in shock. Although well aware of his actions, he somehow could not connect it to the reason for his neighbor's rage.

"What are you doing? What are you talking about?" he asked the intruder.

"Don't play dumb with me, asshole. I've kept my mouth shut about you for too long. I figured we'd be moving soon enough and I'd never have to see your ugly face again, but you have gone too far."

Without warning, Kevin raised his fist and slammed it down into the side of Chandler's cheek. A splatter of blood flew from his mouth, along with one of his yellowed teeth.

"You're lucky Dana called me about the incident instead of Samantha. She's already a wreck, and if she heard about you sneaking into our house and laying in our bed....woooo boy." Kevin looked at the ceiling, thinking about his wife's reaction to hearing about Chandler's intrusion. He raised his hand to strike again, but Chandler put his hands up in a protective position, pleading with him to stop.

As he prepared to unleash another blow, Kevin said, "I should have done this a long time ago. You're lucky I don't feel like losing my job or I would kill you. But whatever you did with that fucking blood on Samantha's pillow... You're sick, man. What are you trying to give her, some kind of disease? I should arrest you for harassment and whatever the fuck you left on her pillow, but I think a good old fashioned ass whooping will be a lot more fun."

Chandler hadn't even considered that the blood from his cheek could have rubbed off when he was lying in their bed. After Dana startled him awake, he left the room quickly without noticing.

Kevin lowered himself and threw a right hook towards his opponent. With Chandler's hands still up in defense, the punch connected with the side of his head rather than his face, saving him from further disfigurement.

"If you need to get laid so badly, go find a prostitute. Samantha's mine."

"You don't deserve her, you fat piece of shit. I hear your arguments every night. She doesn't deserve to be treated that way."

Kevin smiled and said, "Oh, you're finally growing some balls now? You want to speak back to me? When you get your own wife, you can decide how to treat her. I'll treat mine however the fuck I want. In the meantime, you should mind your own business. I can't wait for the day when I'll never have to look at your face again. Freak."

Kevin lowered himself on top of Chandler, his legs straddling the fallen man and pinning him to the floor. The officer grabbed Chandler's arm and pushed it out of the way while he prepared to strike with his other fist.

Chandler panicked. Stuck under the overweight cop and his head still ringing from the previous hits, he had little hope of escaping from underneath the large man. His body tensed as he prepared for the incoming blow. He reached back for anything to defend himself. Clawing against the carpet aimlessly, his hand closed around the first thing it caught hold of, his mother's plastic dinner tray. Chandler brought the tray up toward his assailant at the same time Kevin's fist came down. The punch connected with the tray, knocking the flimsy platter from his hand and out of reach. The initial impact softened the blow to Chandler's face, although it still felt like a brick slamming into his head.

Now Kevin closed his hands around Chandler's throat and tightened his grip. Tears welled up in Chandler's eyes as he struggled for breath. How ironic, he was about to die in the same fashion as his mother did only one day prior. He thought how she was probably watching the scene play out from the heavens, laughing at her son's pitiful performance in the fight for his life.

Chandler's will to fight grew weak and his struggling slowed to a halt. He accepted his fate and resigned himself to death. His final thoughts weren't about Samantha or any of his delusions. He just wanted to be at peace and put an end to his constant misery. With nothing to live for except the guilt of his actions and the weight of his depression, Chandler welcomed the end.

At the last moment, when everything darkened, an unexpected rush of air filled his lungs as his body involuntarily gulped down as much oxygen as it could.

Kevin had released his grip and stood up from his position over him. He loomed over Chandler, who lay gasping for breath, and said, "You're pathetic. Now stay out of our lives."

Humiliated, Chandler seethed at the physical and emotional embarrassment–in his own home, no less. He couldn't let it end this way. Sitting up, he scanned the area around him and set his eyes on the metal fork, discarded from the overturned tray. As Kevin turned to leave, Chandler grabbed the piece of silverware and leaped forward, plunging the utensil deep into the side of Kevin's neck with all his might. The four metal tines punctured the soft underside of Kevin's throat. The fork stuck out of his neck, buried all the way to its roots.

Kevin inhaled as his eyes went wide with shock at the unexpected turn of events. With no time to process what had happened, he twisted back to face Chandler. Trying to make sense of his neighbor's actions, he was unaware of the gravity of his predicament. Instinctively, his hands went to his neck, probing the area where the fork remained implanted in him. He grabbed the handle and pulled, yanking the utensil free.

With the fork free from his throat, blood spurted from the wound like a fountain. Kevin bent over, putting both hands to his neck, and made a croaking sound from deep in his chest. The pressure on his neck slowed the blood flow, but within seconds blood trickled between his fingers. Falling to his knees, Kevin reached for his sidearm, undid the clasp, and pulled it from the holster. His other hand remained pressed against his neck in a futile attempt to stop the blood flow.

His strength waning, the pistol weighed down Kevin's arm and prevented him from taking aim. Unable to raise the weapon, which felt like a lead weight in Kevin's hand, his body swayed back and forth as he sank lower and collapsed on the floor. Within seconds a growing bloodstain spread on the carpet where he fell.

He looked up at Chandler and said, "Please.... Help me," but the sounds that escaped his throat reminded Chandler of someone gargling salt water.

Chandler stood motionless while the police officer struggled, as if viewing the scene of an old movie. His head still rang from the blows he sustained, but he felt no pain. He couldn't feel his body at all. It seemed as if he were floating in the air, formless and looking down on himself as the events unfolded.

Chandler floated and watched as the life drained out of Kevin through the holes in his neck. Four puncture marks in a perfect row. It looked like a vampire with an extra set of fangs had bitten him. He thought of how only moments earlier he had lain on that very same spot, ready and willing to meet his maker.

Then the idea struck him. He was dead. He died with Kevin's hands around his throat. That's why he seemed to hover over the gruesome scene in front of him. Everything after that moment was a dream. To think that he could get the upper hand against a trained officer was laughable. Being dead made perfect sense. It was what he wanted, after all. But then why was Kevin the one lying on the floor, dying in front of him? The questions were overwhelming and made him light headed. The room spun and the walls closed in on him. Chandler's vision clouded as he lost balance, collapsing to the floor next to the dying officer.

Chapter Ten

AFTER AROUSING FROM HIS unplanned nap on the living room floor, Chandler stood in the bathroom and studied himself in the mirror. The skin around his eye had already swollen and turned a dark shade of purple. Tilting his policeman's hat to the side, he attempted to conceal the black eye to the best of his ability. Regardless of the state of his face, he felt invincible. The uniform he wore didn't fit properly, but it gave him a sense of power. He had stripped the outfit from the body in his living room and washed the uniform in the bathroom sink. Despite scrubbing it with a bar of soap to the best of his ability, the bloodstains remained embedded into the fabric. Luckily, the navy blue outfit did a good job of concealing the discoloration.

Moving the body to the basement had taken more effort than he expected. His weakened state and raging nerves caused his arms to tremble as he struggled with the body of the overweight man. His mind compartmentalized the growing number of atrocities under his roof, pushing the horrible memories aside to make way for his own reality. Once he reached the top of the stairs, Chandler took a moment to catch his breath and gave the body a push, letting the corpse tumble end over end to the basement. The repeating thuds from landing on each step ended with a wet crunch when the corpse hit the hard cement floor below. A shiver ran up his spine at the foul sound. The body lay at the bottom with its neck turned at an unnatural angle. It looked back up at Chandler, its eyes wide, as if staring directly at him. He closed the door quickly to rid himself of the view and latched the small lock for good measure.

Unsure what to do with himself, he went back to the living room in his normal spot to look out the window, but the dark red stain on the floor captured his attention. The blood had already begun to congeal, thickening to the consistency of the Greek yogurt his mother occasionally ate. He had the urge to retrieve the cleaning supplies from the kitchen until he remembered that the mess was no longer his problem to deal with. He was either dead or dreaming... or both, and in any of those scenarios, he didn't care about the state of his old house. There was nothing left for him here, and he had no intention of staying.

This dream wasn't like other visions from his night-time slumbers. In normal dreams, he felt like a passenger, just along for the ride, as if sitting in an amusement park attraction on a predetermined track–the metal bar pressed firmly against his lap, a reminder to sit back and enjoy the ride. This, however, seemed more like one of his waking daydreams, except something he couldn't put his finger on felt different from that as well. This felt real, but he knew it couldn't be.

Somewhere in the back of his mind he knew the truth, but his subconscious had buried it so deep that he had no sense of reality. Kevin Reed wouldn't be coming home tonight or ever again. His body lay at the bottom of the basement stairway. To make matters worse, his mother's corpse rested just down the hall, noxious fumes from the first stages of decomposition already wafting throughout the house as a constant reminder of his transgressions. Chandler wished for the usual odor of stale urine and feces. Two people had been killed by his hands in as many days. He didn't like that narrative because he didn't see himself as a killer, so he pushed the truth deeper into the furthest recess of his brain, out of his reach and out of his conscious thoughts.

Instead, he considered this a second chance at life to be a new man. He focused on what he wanted most in the world and who he wanted to be. As he constructed this quintessential existence in his head, he felt like god, sitting at the controls of his own destiny, ready to mold his life into the ideal version that he always dreamed of. Of course, one thing came immediately to mind. The ideal version of his life couldn't be complete without his true love, Samantha. His thoughts traveled back to her, as they always did. He didn't see himself as a selfish man. In fact, he considered himself the opposite. He cared deeply for Samantha and he considered her best interests in the situation. And not just Samantha, but her son Dylan as well.

He knew they weren't happy with the old Kevin, but they didn't deserve to be without a husband and father. That's where he could step in, like a knight in shining armor, and fill that role. With Chandler around, they would be treated like royalty and he'd ensure they lived their best lives.

A vibration on his hip startled Chandler back to reality. The source of the buzzing, along with an electronic version of an old Metallica song, came from a phone clipped to his utility belt. Withdrawing it from the holder, he saw Sam's name flash across the screen. His eyes lit up at the sight of her name, bringing a sense of happiness to him. A text message from his sweetie.

Although it felt like only minutes, it had been hours since his visitor's arrival. During that time, Chandler failed to notice Samantha returning home from work. Glancing at the phone's clock he realized Kevin would usually be home by this time as well.

Opening up the text, he silently mouthed the words to himself as he read the message, "Hey, where are you? Your car was here early but no sign of you. Dinner will be ready in about thirty minutes."

Bringing up the keyboard, he replied, "Sorry. Went down the block to help Pete with something. Be there in a jiffy." He invoked an elderly neighbor who Kevin often helped around the yard with various chores, knowing Samantha wouldn't question it. As soon as he pressed send, Chandler second guessed his choice of worlds.

Jiffy. Who says that? He had one chance to win over Samantha and he was already off on the wrong foot.

Regardless, Chandler had no intentions of wasting his new lease on life. After a hard day at work, he was ready to go home and enjoy a nice, home-cooked meal with his family.

Chapter Eleven

THE RAIN LET UP, slowing to barely a drizzle, but the sky remained overcast, projecting a dark shadow on the street. Chandler watched out the window and waited for the opportune time. The weather kept most people inside, but the occasional car passed by every few minutes, especially at this time in the early evening with people returning home from work. When the street looked clear, he made his move and prayed to remain unseen as he exited the house.

If anyone recognized him wearing a police uniform, they would surely become suspicious. Halloween was still more than six months away, and that was the only rational reason he could think of why he would wear the ridiculous getup.

Keeping close to the house and sticking to the shadows, his heart rate increasing as he crossed to the Reed's property. He hunched low while skirting around Samantha's car parked in the driveway. He felt like a genuine officer about to make a bust on one of those police reality shows as he crept closer to the house. In the end, the walk next door was uneventful, lasting only a few seconds. Relief washed over him as he approached the door, only for his anxiety to return tenfold when it came time to walk through. *What would he say when he walked in? What if Samantha wasn't happy to see him?* He couldn't worry about that now. There was no turning back. He had nothing left to go back to. Besides, this was his home now, and he looked forward to a nice dinner with his family.

Chandler turned the knob to find it unlocked. He had the keys in his pocket but was glad he didn't have to fumble with them and spend any more time on the stoop than necessary.

Inside the house, his senses became immediately overwhelmed with the smell of garlic and tomatoes. He took a deep breath, relishing the pleasant smell. The clinking racket of pots and pans filled his ears as Samantha worked diligently in the kitchen.

Loud pop music with a mesmerizing female voice played from the living room speakers. The singer's passionate vocals repeatedly proclaimed that she was 'bad at love.' Chandler smiled at the lyrics and almost let out an audible laugh. Ironic that a beautiful pop star with an endless supply of suitors would proclaim to be bad at love. Meanwhile, here was Chandler, floundering his way alone through life–but not anymore. Things were finally looking up for him.

Removing his boots by the front door, he crept in quietly as not to disturb the chef. The music covered the sound of his entry, but he maintained a slow, deliberate pace to minimize the chance of a squeaky floorboard giving him away. Noticing Samantha's cell phone sitting on the coffee table alongside a partially full glass of wine, he powered off the phone and slipped it in his back pocket, ensuring no interruptions during their family reunion. He picked up the wine glass and brought it to his nose, whiffing the pungent aroma. He took a small vial out of his pocket and emptied the contents into the glass before setting it back down on the table.

Chandler peered through the archway into the kitchen. Samantha had no inclination of his arrival. Her back to him, she nodded her head in tune to the music while she washed soiled dishes. The reflection of the recessed lights above her shined off her hair. His eyes followed the flowing red hair down her back to the curves of her hips. The tight blue jeans she wore put her perfectly-sized ass on display as she swayed back and forth to the music while scrubbing the crusted pan. Chandler fought the urge to go to her. He wanted to come up behind her and wrap his arms around her waist. He could almost feel the warmth radiating from her body as he squeezed her torso. Samantha would smile at the comfort of their embrace while he nuzzled his face into the crook of her neck.

Although still radiating an aura of confidence, he was not yet ready to face his wife, knowing she wouldn't take kindly to his arrival. Instead, he headed towards another sound. Down the hallway, past the bathroom, he heard a thumping as if someone was throwing books against the wall. He followed the noise to find Dylan in the playroom, jumping on a trampoline with a superhero action figure in each hand.

The boy slowed his jumps to a stop when Chandler came into view. He remained silent with a blank stare at the man in his father's uniform.

"Cool! Is that Green Lantern and Martian Manhunter?" Chandler asked, breaking the silence.

The boy looked at the figures in hand and his eyebrows raised in surprise. "Yes. How do you know that?" he asked.

Chandler laughed. "How wouldn't I know that?" Chandler said. "Those are my favorite members of the Justice League."

Dylan couldn't believe it. In his experience, adults didn't know or care about superheroes. Sometimes his mother would sit and play with him, but she never remembered their names.

Seeing the amazed look on his face, Chandler added, "I love comics. I have a huge collection at my...." he trailed off, flashes of his old life running through his head. Instead, his mind reconciled his new life with the old and continued, "I used to have a huge collection. You're never too old for comic books."

"Do you want to play with me?" the child asked hopefully.

"Sure, I'd love to," Chandler replied with a smile.

With no siblings, Dylan had become accustomed to playing with his favorite toys alone. His dad had little interest in playing with small pieces of plastic. His mom often said he played too rough with the figures. She preferred puzzles or reading books to the boy. Dylan liked those, too, but his favorite was to play heroes and villains with his action figures.

"You have the same uniform as my dad. Do you work with him?" Dylan asked.

Chandler looked down at his clothes, having forgotten about his attire, and then brought his gaze back to the boy and said, "Yeah, something like that. What do you think about me being your dad now?" he asked, seemingly out of nowhere.

Dylan considered the offer for a moment before replying, "Well, I already have a dad, but..." the boy trailed off his sentence, not wanting to say the words.

"Listen, I know he might not be the best dad, but you don't have to worry about that anymore. He had to go away for a while and asked me to come watch after you and your mom."

The child remained silent, unsure how to reply.

Noticing the trepidation in the boy, Chandler added, "How about this? Give me a try for a couple of days and we'll see how it goes. Then you can decide if you want me to stay."

"Okay," said the child and then went directly back to his game. "Here, you be the villains. Take those." He pointed at two figures lying on the carpet beside him.

Chandler stepped in the room and picked up the two figures. He recognized them as The Green Goblin and Thanos. Not the Justice League's usual enemies, but a good matchup, nonetheless.

It seemed the young child needed little convincing to allow Chandler to join the family. He guessed the boy's mother would take considerably more effort to win over. He hoped he was up to the task but for now, he enjoyed playing with the son he always wanted, the son that should be his.

In the kitchen, Samantha removed the chicken parmesan from the oven and checked the clock. Kevin should've been home by now. She appreciated the extra few minutes of peace, but it seemed unlikely for him to miss his favorite meal. She glanced toward the living room for her phone and something odd caught her eye. Kevin's boots sat empty by the front door. She had long ago given up attempting to remind him to take them off inside the house, but the unattended boots alone didn't raise immediate suspicions. That's when she noticed the laughter coming from the playroom. Kevin rarely played toys with Dylan when the boy asked. If it wasn't baseball, football, or another sport, the child usually went ignored. Did he finally give in to the boy's pleas for a playmate? The strangest fact, however, was that her husband hadn't gone straight to the refrigerator to pop open his usual can of beer immediately on returning home from work. Maybe he had turned over a new leaf and things would improve for them. She doubted it, but it couldn't hurt to hope.

Dinner was just about ready, but Samantha hated to interrupt the quality bonding time between the two men in her life. Instead, she crept out to the living room for her wine glass and quickly finished it off before grabbing the bottle from the counter and pouring herself another. She might as well enjoy a few minutes of downtime while the entrée cooled, listening to the music playing in the living room mixed with the laughter coming from down the hall.

She finished plating dinner and set the dishes on the dining room table, crispy chicken parmesan over a bed of angel hair with garlic bread and a side of carrots. Kevin's favorite meal. She hoped the lack of beer plus a home cooked meal would leave her husband in a rare pleasant mood for the night.

"Boys! Dinner's ready!" she yelled down the hall, hoping to catch their attention.

Dylan came running out of the playroom towards her. "Yay, I'm hungry. Did you make spaghetti?" he asked.

"Yes, dear. Go wash your hands and we can eat," she replied.

"Okay. Daddy's friend is coming over for dinner. He'll be right here," the boy added, letting his mother know about his playmate.

She scrunched her nose at the news, unaware of any company coming over for dinner. "Did Dad tell you that? I think he would've told me if I needed to make an extra plate." She looked around for her phone to see if Kevin had texted her about a dinner guest.

"His friend told me. He's in the bathroom now, but don't worry, Dad's not here so you don't need an extra plate."

This statement confused her even more than the first. *What did he mean 'Dad's not here?'*

Noticing the strange look on his mother's face, he grabbed her hand, pulling her towards the kitchen table, and said, "Don't worry, he's really nice. He's a policeman, just like Daddy. He even knows all the superheroes!"

This only caused Samantha's uncertainty to intensify. Her husband wouldn't have a work friend over for dinner if he wasn't going to be there, and Kevin surely would have mentioned it to her. Not wanting to argue with the boy, she allowed him to lead her to the table and took a seat as they waited for the man of the house to join them.

Chapter Twelve

WITH THE FOOD PLATED, mother and son sat impatiently at the kitchen table. The smell of the delicious food only swelled the growling in Dylan's stomach, while Samantha waited for her husband to join them. Eager to find out what her son was talking about, she assumed the boy's tale of her husband's friend joining them for dinner was nothing more than a joke. She couldn't blame the kid for pretending his father was someone else. She often thought about what her life would be like if she had married another man instead of the mean-spirited husband with whom she shared a name. Even with Dylan's warning, she couldn't have been more surprised when Chandler turned the corner and came into view.

Startled at seeing her neighbor walking into her kitchen like he owned the place, she immediately asked the obvious question. "What are you doing here?"

He smiled and replied nonchalantly, as if his appearance was nothing out of the ordinary. "Hey hun, it smells delicious. I haven't had a good home-cooked meal in forever. It looks great. Thanks for cooking."

Stunned at his response, she didn't know how to reply. Feeling like she stepped into an alternate universe, the first thought that popped into her head was that she couldn't remember the last time Kevin thanked her for cooking dinner. Regardless of the compliment, Samantha stood up from her chair in utter shock.

"I'm not sure what this is, but if Kevin sees you here he will kill you, and I'm not exaggerating," she said. With the surprise of seeing Chandler in her house, she hadn't even noticed the uniform he wore or the streaks of maroon that entwined the fabric of his shirt.

Chandler replied, feeling more confident than ever in his new persona. "Oh, don't worry about him. He won't be joining us this evening. We're going to try something new. Dylan seemed quite happy when I told him I'd be staying with you."

At that point, it clicked in Samantha's head that the intruder had already been inside her home for who knew how long. The entire time she sat and sipped her wine, listening to her son's laughter from down the hall, this man, who was clearly having a mental breakdown, was with him. She looked at her son to confirm his well-being. He sat in his chair nibbling on the garlic bread while he waited for Chandler to join them. He looked the same as ever, without a care and fearless of the situation–just a normal day in the Reed household.

Noticing his mom's shocked stare, he smiled at her and said, "It's okay Mom, he's nice. He's from next door." Then he turned to Chandler and added, "Sit down, I'm hungry."

Samantha, dumbfounded by the situation, remained silent, unsure of what to say. With no argument from her, Chandler accepted the boy's invitation to sit at the table at the spot opposite Samantha, allowing his gaze to meet hers across the table.

Chandler watched her intently, waiting for her next response. This would be the true test for him. Would she accept the sudden change to her family? He felt that, deep down, she had no love for her former husband, but he knew that such a drastic change would be hard to accept. For that reason, he was willing and prepared to give her time to adjust. How much time it would take her he didn't know, but Chandler was a patient man and he would do whatever it took to make sure they were a happy family.

They sat in silence, locked in a staring contest as if they were two animals vying to prove dominance over the other. The tension in the room was so thick the air became hard to breathe. Samantha was used to tension between her and her husband, but this felt like something right out of the twilight zone.

She looked over at her son, who had begun eating. A tangle of spaghetti hung from his mouth. He slurped up the noodles, allowing a large glob of tomato sauce to fall back to his plate as he inhaled the dangling pasta. She marveled at how the boy could continue going on as if nothing out of the ordinary was happening. She wished for the innocent ignorance of a child, but she knew she had to act.

Samantha looked around the room for her phone. *Where did she put it?* Without seeing the device anywhere in reach, her eyes drifted toward the front door. She considered grabbing her son and making a dash for it. She pictured herself flipping the table over and catching Chandler completely off guard. *Would the flying dishes and food distract him long enough to make it outside?* Alone she might have risked it, but she knew she'd never be able to get Dylan out before Chandler intervened.

Instead, she relied on her usual method of dulling the awkward tension from her life. She picked up her wineglass and closed her eyes while she took a large gulp of the red liquid inside. As the wine warmed her belly, she wondered if she made a mistake by continuing to drink with that man in her home. She already felt the effects of the first glass.

"Should you really be drinking in your condition?" Chandler asked.

"My condition?" she replied. "What do you mean?"

"Sorry, your realtor spilled the secret about your little bun in the oven," he said.

With a look of confusion on her face, she said, "I don't know what you're talking about, but that's not true." Her words were already slurring from the effects of her wine.

She closed her eyes and smiled at the ridiculous notion of having another baby while stuck in that awful relationship. Even if it were possible, she wouldn't do that to another child. With her eyes closed, she lost her equilibrium for a split second, almost falling out of the chair until she opened them again.

Chandler picked up his fork and twirled the pasta before bringing it to his mouth, giving a grunt of approval as he tasted the dish. Even while eating Chandler watched her like a hawk, keeping his eyes trained on her. Samantha looked at her utensils but refused to ignore the situation. She couldn't just eat dinner as if everything was normal. She didn't want to make a scene in front of her son, either, but it seemed inevitable.

"Dylan, please go to your room. I need to talk with Mr. Chandler."

"But mom, I'm not done eating," he replied.

Chandler cut in as if daring Samantha to overrule him and said, "It's okay Dylan, we're a family now and anything your mother has to say can be said in the open. We shouldn't have any secrets from each other."

She couldn't believe her ears. Did this man really think he belonged here? That they were a family? She didn't know what was going on in his mind, but there was no denying the fact that he was bat shit crazy. He couldn't just walk into their lives and be a part of their family. She'd lived next to Chandler for years and always knew him as the passive, shy type. This intrusion seemed very out of character for him. More annoyed and angry than scared of him, she asked again, "Where is Kevin? What is going on?"

"I know this might be hard for you to hear, but I've seen the way he treats you and, more importantly, Dylan. I hear the yelling every night. He doesn't deserve a family like yours, and it's time you understand what it's like to be with someone who loves and protects you. Give it some time and you'll see how much better things will be this way. Just give me a chance to make you happy."

This couldn't be happening. His words rang true, but not like this. She tried to scream but her mouth didn't want to open. She tried to stand but felt weighed down, as if her body had turned into sandbags. Her arms and legs disobeyed her commands like they were glued to the chair. A bout of dizziness rushed over her. She felt like she was about to faint. Panic finally set in as she lost all control of her motor functions.

The imposter watched intently as various escape plans cycled through Samantha's head. Being a master of hypothetical scenarios, it was as if he knew her every thought. He saw the quick glances she stole at the door. The fact that she hadn't run or screamed at the first sight of him confirmed his plan could work. The door was in view, yet she remained seated at the table. She had to know she wasn't in any danger. He would never harm her or Dylan. Samantha's adjustment period might be even quicker than he hoped. Maybe his initial precautions were unnecessary, but he always remembered the Boy Scout motto from his tenure with the organization as a child. It was an adage he took to heart ever since his scout leaders ingrained the two-word phrase into him so many years ago. Be prepared.

He came prepared for the worst but hoped for the best. So far, he couldn't have asked for a more favorable outcome. It's not like he expected her to run over and greet him with a kiss, although that would have been fantastic. Regardless of how lost in his delusions he became, he grounded his expectations in reality.

He watched as Samantha slumped over in her chair, still trying to talk but barely able to string her words together into anything intelligible. Her head lolled to one side as she struggled to remain upright. It would only be another minute until she slipped away from consciousness. The drugs he slipped into her wine glass when he first entered the house had worked their way through her body, dulling her sense of reality.

Samantha knew something was wrong. She shouldn't feel this way after only two glasses of wine. Fear finally kicked in as she realized the severity of her situation. Looking towards Dylan, she tried to tell him to run, but the sounds came out muffled and garbled together. She saw herself tipping in her chair but could do nothing to prevent the inevitable fall. She drifted off to sleep before her head even hit the wooden floor as she toppled over.

Watching his mother fall to the ground, Dylan looked fearfully at Chandler, hoping for a cue. Seeing the boy's worried look, Chandler simply said, "Dylan, your mom's not feeling well tonight. I'm gonna help her to bed so she can get some rest."

Chapter Thirteen

SAMANTHA'S EYES FLUTTERED BUT remained closed as she crept back towards consciousness. Her head pounded, as if a jackhammer was chiseling away at a crack in her skull. Thoughts washed over her in waves, fighting each other for attention, but the pain in her head prevented any of them from coming into focus. *What a strange dream. I need to lay off the wine. What even happened last night? The last thing I remember was filling up my wine glass before dinner.*

The sun had just crept over the horizon, and although the curtains blocked most of the morning light, the edges were illuminated by the glow of the day. Finally her eyes opened, but even in the mostly darkened room pain seared into her brain as if a lazer were burning scorch marks in her skull. Even the small amount of light increased the magnitude of her migraine tenfold. She heard a voice but it sounded far off in the distance.

"I was hoping you'd wake up soon. We have a lot to talk about. How are you feeling?"

Samantha blinked her eyes repeatedly, taking in her surroundings but seeing nothing more than dancing shadows on the walls. The pain began to subside, only to be replaced by nausea. Attempting to sit up and wipe a string of drool from her mouth, she pulled on her arm but it refused to obey her commands.

"Try to relax. This is just a precaution while we talk things out. It's for your own protection. You have nothing to worry about. I would never hurt you. You know that."

Samantha tried to clear her head but felt her brain drowning in mud. The walls of her mind collapsed around her as she attempted to dig out of the hole, but the more she struggled the faster the dirt closed in on her, preventing oxygen from reaching her lungs.

The restraints holding her arms in place rustled against the bedposts as she struggled to move her arms. The soft texture of the bands around her wrists tickled while she worked at the cuffs to no avail.

"I found those in a box under the bed. I hope you don't mind. I figured they would be more comfortable than the metal ones. They look pretty durable. I think they should hold you."

This can't be real. It's just a dream. I'm hallucinating. Her thoughts swirled as the shadow stood up and walked to the window, opening the shades slowly to let more light enter the room.

As the light poured in, she squinted at the change in brightness while her eyes adjusted and confirmed what she already knew. The man standing before her was not her husband, Kevin, but their next door neighbor Chandler. Still trying to make sense of the situation while dealing with the lingering effects of the narcotics, she realized she was a captive in her own home. Samantha felt defenseless and exposed, like standing naked in front of a stranger. But she wasn't naked and this man wasn't a stranger, not completely anyway.

Instead of the jeans and knit sweater she wore last night, she had on a peach satin nightgown from her drawer. Looking over at Chandler, she immediately recognized the silk pajamas her husband usually slept in. This man seemingly stepped right into her husband's life and replaced him without a second thought. She marveled at the notion that he expected everyone else to just go along with the fantasy.

He watched while she inspected their clothing and felt like he could read her mind. The notion of being so in-tune with each other that he knew her every thought only solidified his belief that they were true soulmates. Meaning to assuage her fears he said, "You were so tired last night you didn't even finish your dinner. After you fell asleep I got you up to bed and helped you slip into something more comfortable. I hope that's okay. I mean, who sleeps in jeans, right? I guess you had a little bit too much to drink, but don't worry, I took care of you. It's nothing to be embarrassed about, it happens to everyone. And before you go getting all worried, nothing happened. Scout's honor. I mean, I couldn't help taking a little peak–can you blame me? But that's it, and it's nothing I haven't seen before anyway, although it's been too long." Chandler cracked a smile at the last statement, picturing her naked body.

Listening to the man's creepy words, she panicked. She had to get out of there. If she could make it to the street to wave down a passing car or even get outside long enough to scream for help she could attract a nearby neighbor, anyone that could save her from this monster. But she couldn't escape. Not while she was handcuffed to the bed. Instead, she spoke, trying to muster an authoritative tone, but her voice came out quivering. "I... I don't know what you think this is, but you need to let me go right now."

"I'm sorry Samantha, but this is for your own good. It's like one of those things you see on TV... what's it called? An intervention. Plus, you hit your head pretty badly when you fell. I couldn't just leave you. I had to make sure you were okay. Anyway, I already texted my boss and told him I wasn't going to be in to work today, so we'll have all day together."

"Your boss? What are you talking about? Where is my son?"

The pain subsided, but the onslaught of unanswered questions did little to soothe the confusion in Samantha's head. Fragments of the previous night came back to her. She vaguely remembered sitting at the dinner table, being unable to control her body, and then nothing. It's as if she skipped forward in time, bypassing the remainder of the night to awaken bound to her bed the next morning.

"Tell me what the fuck is going on!" she yelled, raising her voice in an attempt to exert a false sense of control.

"Please. Keep your voice down. Dylan is still sleeping. You don't want to wake him. I don't think he should see you like this."

"I don't care about my voice, just untie me right now!"

Chandler looked at her and sighed. This might not be as easy as he was hoping after all. He hated the need to restrain Samantha, but her words made it clear she couldn't be trusted to behave herself.

"Listen, I know this must be strange and even a little frightening, but you have nothing to worry about. How about this? I'll take Dylan to daycare, and when I return, we'll be free to talk and get to know each other a little better. I'm sure after a few hours alone together you'll understand that we share a connection. We're soulmates."

Samantha didn't know what to say. This man had clearly gone off the deep end, but one thing he said made sense. Getting her son out of the house and to the safety of his daycare was the highest priority. Then she could think of a way to fight back or escape without needing to worry about the boy.

Just as her thoughts came together, focusing on getting the child out of the house, the bedroom door creaked open to reveal Dylan standing in the doorway. His fingers clenched the ear of his tattered, blue monkey while the rest of the stuffy dangled back and forth, brushing against the floor as it swung.

The boy spoke softly, still in a daze from his night's rest. "Mom? Are you feeling better today?"

She felt the urge to scream for him to help but knew there was nothing he could do. She wished she could give him a message for the teachers or slip a note in his bag, but being tied to the bed and with Chandler in the room, her options were limited.

Chandler replied to calm the boy's fears. "She's okay. She just needs a day to rest and I'm sure she'll be back to her old self by tomorrow. Isn't that right, Sam? I'm going to stay here with her today to make sure she gets better."

The boy's eyes lit up. "I wanna stay home too. I can help Mommy feel better."

Now it was Samantha's turn to reply. Her throat cracked as she tried to speak, reminding her of her tongue's desperate need for moisture. She forced the dry air through her vocal cords and said, "Listen to this man. He's going to take you to school. When you get there, just tell them that mom needs..."

Chandler cut her off before she put any ideas in the boy's head. "You can just tell them Mom's good friend dropped you off today because she needed a little break." He turned to Samantha and added, "Isn't that right?"

She knew arguing was pointless, and her primary concern was for the well-being of her child, so she agreed and turned her head, closing her eyes and wishing the situation away. She didn't want her son to see her like this.

The boy looked at his mother and knew something was wrong. He heard it in her voice and saw it in the way she struggled on the bed. Dylan hated being sick and imagined the pain his mom must be feeling. He ran to her and put his arms around her waist, gripping her in a tight squeeze. He hoped the big hug would help her feel better, but he knew the nice man from next door would take good care of her.

"Your breakfast is on the table. I hope you like waffles," Chandler said to the boy.

The mere mention of waffles had Dylan out of the bedroom and speeding down the stairs towards the kitchen. His poor mother, sick in bed and unable to get up, was already a fading memory in the back of his mind.

Chapter Fourteen

"Be right back, sweetie. Don't go anywhere."

That was the last thing the man impersonating her husband said as he leaned over to kiss her on the cheek before leaving with her son. The words rang in Samantha's head like a bell tower, echoing back and forth inside her mind as she lay helpless in bed.

This can't be happening. Where is Kevin? This can't be happening. Her thoughts raced from one fear to the next and back again. Fragmented memories flashed in her mind as she gradually remembered more details from the previous night, but anything after dinner was a blank.

She had no recollection of coming upstairs nevermind being strapped to the bed. She pictured her limp body being carried (dragged?) up the stairs to her bed. Although she kept herself in decent shape, she was no toothpick and probably even weighed a few pounds more than Chandler. She imagined him struggling to move her lifeless body while Dylan watched.

As she racked her brain, trying to focus and fill in the missing memories, the pain in her head returned. The dull throb beat in tune with her heart. Thump.

Thump. Thump. Whatever Chandler used to drug her sure packed a wallop. She must have been out for at least ten hours. What did Dylan do during all that time? She couldn't imagine him cooperating for Chandler when Kevin couldn't even get the boy to bed on his own. The child seemed fine this morning, though. Even with Chandler's delusions, she didn't think he would hurt the child. The man just wanted to be accepted and loved, not to hurt anyone. She had to believe that.

Finally, her thoughts settled on something else that had been nagging at her. She tried to ignore the fact that Chandler must have gone through the dresser to find her outfit and changed her clothes while she was unconscious. It was hardly her go-to selection of cotton pajamas; she only broke out this outfit when trying to be sexy for Kevin. Her current mood left her feeling anything but. Chandler could have done anything to her while she was unconscious, and she would never know. She didn't feel violated, but her whole body still tingled from being drugged and she couldn't be sure.

Where was Kevin anyway? Although she refused to admit the truth, subconsciously she knew Kevin wouldn't be coming to save her. Not now or ever. Chandler seemed confident that nothing would interrupt their dinner. She noticed the bloodstains on Chandler's shirt, even if she refused to come to terms with it at the time. No, not on Chandler's shirt, on Kevin's uniform. *How else would he be wearing that uniform?* Deep down, Samantha knew her husband was dead, but without proof she held out hope. Either way, she couldn't think about that right now. She had to focus on herself. Waiting around for someone to save her wasn't an option. If she wanted to get out of this mess, she couldn't rely on anyone but herself.

She tried to think, but her head swam from the lingering effects of the drugs. A bout of nausea roiled her stomach. She felt a hunger pain in her belly but was glad not to have eaten dinner the previous night; she would probably be laying in a pile of her own vomit.

She felt the bed bobbing up and down as if floating in the open ocean and knew trying to stand would be an unsuccessful endeavor. It's not like she could right herself anyway, with the leather cuffs around her wrists shackling her to the bed. Instead, she focused on her stomach and quelling her nausea. *Calm down. Just breathe. I'm okay. It could be worse. Breathe in, breathe out.* She repeated these short phrases to herself.

For the first time since the intruder entered her home, Samantha had a reprieve from the emotional onslaught brought on by fear and stress. Her mind still raced with worry and thick beads of sweat dripped down the side of her brow, but she took slow deep breaths in and out to calm herself and clear her mind. *In through your nose, out through your mouth. Think of tall grass, swaying in a light breeze.* As her body relaxed, her heart rate decreased. All those years of Tuesday night yoga classes were finally paying off. She took a moment to assess the situation.

Now that she was no longer hyperventilating, and with her body temperature decreasing, she realized she was laying in a puddle of sweat. It wasn't as bad as vomit, but it was still uncomfortable. The sudden change in body temperature jarred her senses. Her satin nightgown was soaked completely through and stuck to her skin as she writhed in place on the bed. A dark ring surrounded her where the moisture had seeped through her clothes to the sheets below, creating a damp outline of her form.

The cool sweat coating her body caused a shiver to run along her spine. Lying in the pool of perspiration with no way to dry out, she resigned herself to the uncomfortable position. Instead, Samantha attempted to use the moisture for her benefit. Looking at the binding holding her, she saw the leather straps were different from handcuffs in that there was no key. Instead, a heavy-duty buckle secured the leather braces. She hoped her sweat-slicked skin would allow her to wiggle free from the restraint.

Twisting her wrist back and forth while contracting her thumb, Samantha applied pressure on the cuff while pulling on her arm. She took a deep breath and prayed the moist leather would stretch as she increased the force, allowing her wrist to slip through. She only needed to free one of her hands to escape, but the more she struggled against the binding, the tighter it felt. Regardless of the increasing pain, she continued twisting her wrist while applying pressure on her arm. The friction inflamed her wrist and irritated her skin from the repeated motion, but no matter which direction she struggled, the buckle remained tight. With even the slightest amount of swelling, she'd have no hope of slipping out of the bonds. Out of frustration, Samantha flailed both arms in the air as far as her bracelets allowed.

She cursed Kevin for getting the top of the line BDSM restraints. A cheaper set would have been easier to wiggle her way out of or or even break but with Kevin being a police officer, he insisted on only using the best hardware. The illusion of helplessness wasn't enough for him. He demanded genuine shackles for their intimate encounters, probably fulfilling some deep-seated fantasy from his time working as a corrections officer. With these bonds, she had little chance of undoing them on her own, and Samantha thought she might dislocate her arm before squeezing out of them. At least Chandler was right, they were more comfortable than the metal police handcuffs. After using Kevin's work-issued pair a few times for recreation years ago, they both quickly agreed to get a more pleasant set for play. Although, their current use could hardly be construed as entertainment.

She thought of the Stephen King movie with the woman in a similar predicament. Kevin put it on for one of his selections on movie night. Of course if it involved bondage, it was right up Kevin's alley. It was ironic considering her current position at the hands of her neighbor. Hoping she wouldn't have to resort to the extreme measures in the film to free herself, she considered her options. Break her wrist in an attempt to escape? Samantha didn't think she had it in her. *Wait. Stop, you're getting ahead of yourself.* The lady in the movie was left alone for days with no one coming to help. Samantha only had a few minutes before Chandler returned. It's not like he would leave her to die. Not quite the same situation, even though it felt like it.

Chandler left in her car to take Dylan to daycare and wouldn't be gone long. Ten minutes to the daycare, five minutes to drop him off, and ten minutes back home. She wondered how drop off would go. She normally liked to see Dylan settled and playing with friends before leaving him for the day. Now her special boy was at the whim of a madman. The workers at the preschool were more than competent and she trusted Dylan in their care, as long as they made it to daycare. For the first time, she considered the possibility that Chandler could just drive off with Dylan and never be seen again. She couldn't bear the thought, however unlikely the scenario seemed. She had to trust that Dylan was safe and Chandler would be returning shortly. After all, if the man really believed he was her husband, he had no reason to flee.

Although she could see the clock on the nightstand, she hadn't been paying attention to the time when they left. She'd be lucky to have ten more minutes until he returned. She didn't put up a fight when he left with her son since the boy would be safer at the center than home with them. Not having the boy to worry about would simplify any attempt to escape or fight. Fight. She'd barely considered the possibility until now. Every time she thought about escaping, it involved running and fleeing the house, hoping to find someone on the street to assist before the lunatic clobbered her from behind.

The scene played out in her head like an old horror movie. She pictured herself being dragged across the street by her hair, the psychopath bringing her back inside the house only to chop her up into pieces. But this wasn't a horror movie and Chandler Hendricks wasn't Michael Myers. He didn't want to kill her; he wanted to marry her, and although he had quite the strange method of courting a woman, she thought about how she could use it to her advantage.

He didn't seem like the average psychopath, not that she knew many psychopaths, but the Chandler she knew from years ago wouldn't hurt a fly. How had he strayed so far from reality that his life became reduced to this?

If she was unable to free herself, she would have to convince Chandler to release her. That meant playing along with his sick fantasy until she found an opening. Although she cringed at the thought of being a willing participant in his delusion, doing so would be her best chance to escape. After all, she wouldn't get very far while chained to the bed.

Samantha scooched herself back against the headboard until she felt the sensation of the cold wood against her exposed shoulders. Her body appreciated the new position, even if the muscles in her arms ached from being held outstretched for such a long period. She looked towards the window. If the shades were completely open, her new vantage point would have given her a view of the street. With them mostly closed, she could barely make out the moving shadow of a car as it passed by.

Running out of options and time, Samantha resorted to her last hope. It was something she should have tried the moment Chandler drove off in her car. Being on the second floor of her house, it seemed unlikely anyone could hear her screaming, especially with the windows closed, but she had to try.

"Help! Anyone! Please! Help me!" she screamed at the top of her lungs, knowing someone would need to be basically on her property for any chance of hearing her pleas.

The screaming instantly reminded her of how dry her mouth was. She could feel the tendons in her throat crack with each syllable that escaped her lips. What she wouldn't give for a sip of water. Now that the need for a drink filled her mind, her thirst increased with each passing moment. She had half a mind to suck some of her perspiration from the sheets, but she doubted she would have much success. Why hadn't she asked Chandler for a drink before he left? At the time, it hadn't even occurred to her. Regardless of her parched mouth, she continued to scream for help, as if her life depended on it.

Chapter Fifteen

Celine Foster pressed the doorbell a second time and followed it immediately with a knock on the door. Her patience had already grown thin from being threatened and then brushed off the day before. Now the man-child had her waiting forever on the stoop of her friend's house. Chandler never left the house, so he was obviously home and ignoring her. After their awkward confrontation the previous day, Celine had grown considerably more concerned for her housebound friend.

She had half a mind not to return at all to avoid another encounter with the man. As much as Celine cared for Rose, this was not the first time she considered abandoning her. Throughout the years, she watched her friend's son grow from a boy into a man, and, from an outside perspective, Celine saw what her friend could not.

Something wasn't right with Rose's son. Celine thought he acted as if a switch inside his brain was flipped the wrong way. She noticed the strange behavior ever since he was a young boy. She only dared broach the subject with her friend a few times over the years and was met with hostility and scorn on each occasion. She didn't blame Rose. Most mothers refused to see the faults in their children, no matter how obvious the flaw. Instead, her maternal instinct overrode common sense and she refused to believe her little angel could be anything other than perfect.

His odd quirks as a young child turned into bizarre obsessions as a teenager. Celine had known about his unstable personality for years and should have acted long ago, but out of respect for the family she remained silent. Now, with Rose confined to her bed, she depended on her son for everything, and after yesterday's interaction, Celine could remain silent no longer.

She knew the boy's multitude of problems stemmed from his father abandoning them, although she admitted Rose's poor handling of the situation didn't do the child any favors. She hadn't seen Chandler's dad in nearly thirty years but would never forget the smug know-it-all attitude he exhumed with every breath he took. The rules never applied to men like him, so it wasn't much of a surprise when he went out for a hypothetical carton of milk and never came back. As a new mom, Rose took it hard. Who wouldn't? But Celine's empathy for Rose and the child became a catalyst for their friendship.

The lack of a father figure in the boy's life only exacerbated his predisposed mental issues that were surely inherited from his birth father. The common phrase about the apple and the tree came to mind.

Celine didn't know which would be worse, growing up without a father or growing up with *that* father. Either way, he was gone and Chandler suffered for it. Years later, Celine attempted to convince her friend to look for a new man and move on, maybe even marry again, but Rose was so crushed by her husband's betrayal she gave up all interest in men and romance. From that point on, Chandler became the only man to occupy her heart and thoughts.

When Celine learned that at twelve years old Chandler still slept in his mother's bed, she became concerned, not only for the boy, but for his mother as well. Rose brushed it off, mentioning the boy's horrible night terrors. Apparently, the child believed monsters lurked in the shadows of his room, waiting to gobble him up as soon as he closed his eyes. Instead of helping the boy understand the truth about his irrational fears, she allowed these thoughts to fester while she welcomed him into her empty bed. Although strictly a platonic relationship, she used him as a warm body and companion to replace the husband who left her. She never noticed that her need to replace Chandler's father did irreparable harm to his already precarious mental state.

Although Celine harbored no ill-will towards Chandler, he emitted an off-putting aura, upsetting the natural balance of his surroundings. Celine had spent a lot of time meditating, learning to be at peace with nature. Anytime she came in close proximity to Chandler she felt negative energy radiating off of him.

She preferred to avoid the strange man at all costs. The ever growing dark cloud that hung over him was a major reason for the decline of Celine's friendship with Rose. Celine could barely stand to be near him, and after his threatening gesture the day before, it was a miracle she had even come back at all. She considered calling the police right then and there, but he seemed so apologetic after realizing his mistake she decided to let it go and check back in again today.

Now, standing at the door knocking repeatedly with no response, she wondered if she made a mistake waiting this long. After watching the altercation between the neighbors yesterday, she understood that Chandler's nerves got the best of him when they spoke. Although the man clearly had issues, he didn't seem like the violent type. Still, she had a nagging feeling in the back of her mind that he was spiraling out of control. With Rose bedridden, it felt like Chandler would reach his breaking point soon. Celine knew that if she didn't intervene, no one else would.

If only Celine's eyesight hadn't been deteriorating, she would've seen the dark red stain stamped into the carpet through the small window next to the door. Chandler hadn't bothered cleaning up the mess and left the blood to coagulate into the rug. But Celine took no notice of the stained interior and instead focused her attention on the flowerbeds along the front of the house while she waited. Being an avid gardener, it pained her to see the plants left unattended. A few still bloomed, but weeds had overtaken many while vines choked off others. Ready to give up on receiving a response, Celine turned away from the Hendricks house and proceeded back down the path. Returning home without seeing her friend, she wondered how she could help Rose if she couldn't even get in to see her.

Although Celine's eyesight had seen better days, unlike many of her geriatric peers, she still had the ears of a cat. If given the choice, she would have kept her perfect vision over her hearing, but as her vision declined, her hearing seemed to heighten. Being home alone for so many years, she became accustomed to a quiet house and any small noise would interrupt her concentration.

This day, her keen hearing picked up the faintest cry as she walked across the yard away from her friend's house. Unsure if the sound came from a person, an animal, or an errant television set, she stopped in her tracks and perked up her ears to listen for the noise. Just as she was about to chalk the cry up to a noisy TV or neighbor's stubbed toe, she heard it again. This time, ready and waiting for the sound, she made out the noise more clearly and knew instantly the voice belonged to a human. Her first instinct was that her friend needed help, but after tilting her head to hone in on the direction of the cry, she realized the sound didn't emulate from Rose's house but the home next door. Just like the other neighbors in the vicinity, Celine was accustomed to odd noises coming from the Reed household at all hours of the night. It was no secret the way Mr. Reed treated his wife. In other circumstances, she might have involved herself in their quarrels for the poor woman's sake, but she knew better than to make a domestic complaint against a police officer. No matter how bad she felt for his wife, Celine didn't want to risk becoming a target herself.

Hearing the noise at this hour in the morning, when Mr. Reed should be at work, raised an alarm inside Celine. It sounded like a call for help. If the poor woman had fallen or hurt herself while home alone and couldn't reach her phone, she could be lying helpless on the floor for hours before anyone found her. She thought of herself in the same situation and couldn't bear going back home with the chance that Samantha needed assistance. Although later she might come to regret it, Celine decided to investigate the call for help. If it was just a misunderstanding and Mrs. Reed wasn't in distress, maybe they'd have a laugh about it. Missing her long talks with Rose, Celine just wanted someone to chat with, even if only for a couple of minutes, and this was the perfect excuse to check in on her other neighbor.

Chapter Sixteen

THE DROP OFF AT daycare went easier than expected. Chandler knew the name of the center and pulled up the directions on the car's GPS. Bracing himself for an awkward conversation with the teachers, he reverted to his usual reserved self and let Dylan take the lead. Luckily, the boy was all too happy to be in charge and raced down the hallway to show Chandler his classroom. To Chandler's surprise, a quick glance from the adults in the room was the most attention they received.

The young ladies working at the daycare already looked overwhelmed by the other children running rampant and clearly hadn't had their morning coffee yet. Dylan made a dash for the cubbies against the wall and pointed out the one with his name on it. After depositing his lunch and supplies for the day, the boy gave Chandler a hug and went directly to the pile of toys in the center of the floor, joining the makeshift game already in progress. None of the teachers questioned his relationship to the boy or even said anything to him other than a quick nod and half smile as he stood in the corner for a minute watching the children play.

Taking this as a good sign, Chandler slipped out of the room before drawing any more attention to himself and headed back to Samantha's Subaru. Before starting the car and heading home, he took a minute to consider how well the drop off had gone. Hell, his whole time with Dylan had been great. People always said taking care of a child was harder than it looked, but it seemed he was catching on quickly. Chandler related to the boy in a way that no one else could. The boy was so starved for positive attention from his father that he took to Chandler almost immediately. After getting Samantha to bed last night, he helped Dylan change into his pajamas, brush his teeth, and even read him a book from the boy's shelf. Yes, things were going really well with Dylan, and it gave Chandler a sense of pride and meaning in his life. Now if he could only get the boy's mother to respond the same way.

Chandler's ever-increasing anxiety and agoraphobia had kept him from driving a car in years. Although in some ways driving was like riding a bike–once you learn, you'll never forget—he felt uncomfortable behind the wheel for the first time in so long. With Dylan strapped to the car seat in the back, he felt responsible for the child's well-being and took every precaution for his safety on the ride. During the ten minute drive to the preschool, Chandler's deliberately slow pace infuriated the other drivers behind him while he focused his complete attention on the road ahead.

Now, without a child in the backseat to worry about, Chandler slowly regained his confidence behind the wheel and picked up his speed in his excitement to get back to Samantha. Passing by several lightly wooded areas intermixed with shopping centers and strip malls, he took in the sights of his town, surprised by how much the area had changed in such a short time. As he got closer to home, he passed through a number of residential neighborhoods, most looking virtually identical to his own.

Chandler's eagerness to return to his love outweighed his thoughts of safety as he pressed harder on the gas pedal. He couldn't leave Samantha waiting too long for him. He laughed at the thought. Having a beautiful woman waiting at home in bed was something he never thought would apply to him. Proud at overcoming his anxiety and looking forward to spending time with his wife, Chandler beamed. Plastered on his face was a big smile for other drivers to see as they passed by. Breaking out of his shell had helped him achieve his lifelong dream and changed his future for the better. *If only Mother could see me now.*

About half the distance back to his wife, a loud bell rang out that sounded like it came from inside the car. The dashboard reverberated from a buzzing that accompanied the noise. The sound broke Chandler's concentration, startling him. His hand jerked the wheel at the unexpected ringing, causing the car to hit the curb and jostling him even more. He pressed on the brake and regained control of the vehicle before it crashed.

Chandler realized the source of the obnoxious sound was Kevin's cell phone, which sat in the dashboard cubby.

Compared to Kevin's usual Metallica ringtone, this clinical sound was as annoying as the sound of an early morning alarm clock. Pulling into a parking lot, Chandler grabbed the phone to look for the source of the buzzing and silence it. He hoped it wasn't an urgent call from the police department requesting him to work. He already texted the chief, letting him know he felt under the weather and wouldn't be in today.

Looking at the phone, the face he saw came as a surprise. A picture of his mother's friend Celine filled the screen. No, not a picture, a video. She seemed to be only inches from the camera, but looking away, off to the side. Confused at what he saw, he considered why this lady's image was being transmitted to his phone.

Three buttons appeared along the bottom of the frame. Reply with audio, reply with video and ignore. Wondering why Kevin would get a call from his elderly neighbor, he hesitated before making a selection when he heard the woman speak. Her voice echoed on the phone's small speaker, as if she were shouting to someone far away,

"Hello? Is anyone there? Are you okay?" she said directly into the camera before her.

Chandler remained quiet, but after a moment Celine's facial expression changed suddenly, as if the woman heard a shocking sound. Then he saw her reach forward and fumble with something next to the camera before advancing out of sight.

With Celine gone from the camera, Chandler had a better view of the background and saw the old woman's house in the rear of the frame. This only confused him more as he tried to picture the signal's source. Studying the image closer, he recognized the mailbox that he checked every day for most of his life in the corner. He thought of his interaction with Celine the day before and suddenly remembered that she said she would return today. Was he somehow looking out his own front door? No, the angle wasn't right. Then he remembered the doorbell camera on the Reed's house. Celine was there right now! Samantha must have been calling for help. How stupid could he be? Chandler kicked himself for not putting a gag in her mouth before leaving the woman alone. He thought they were earning each other's trust, but apparently, they still had a long way to go. Panicking, Chandler pressed his foot on the accelerator and sped home as fast as he could.

Chapter Seventeen

MRS. REED'S CRIES FOR help became clearer when Celine reached the woman's front door. So clear, in fact, Samantha was able to shout down instructions for the lockbox left by the realtor for her showings. Luckily, Samantha knew the combination to access the key, giving Celine an easy way in the house.

After entering the code, the box popped open, revealing the prize inside. If not for the accessible key, Celine would have had no other choice but to wait outside and call the police for help. In hindsight, calling emergency services might have been a better option, but unaware of the seriousness of Samantha's predicament, she couldn't leave her neighbor in peril while they waited for a patrol car if another option existed. Celine never considered she could be putting herself in any danger in the process. With the key in hand, she unlocked the front door and entered the house to help her distressed neighbor.

Thinking of her own worst fear, she expected to find Mrs. Reed on the floor with a broken leg or hip preventing the poor woman from reaching her phone.

She followed the sound of Samantha's calls leading her through the house. Living alone as an older woman, Celine had long feared finding herself in this scenario. Knowing her anxiety at being alone all day, her children purchased a LifeAlert bracelet for her in case she found herself in an emergency such as this. As of yet she'd never needed to use it, but having the device strapped to her wrist at all times gave her a peace of mind that she wouldn't have without it.

Hearing the cry from the second floor, Celine climbed the stairs toward Samantha's voice as fast as her geriatric legs allowed. Unfortunately, because of her advanced age, Celine's top speed was excruciatingly slow.

"Samantha, are you okay? Hold on, I'm coming," she yelled as she ascended the steps.

"Please hurry," came the reply. "We don't have much time."

Celine didn't know what she meant by the last statement, but she paid it little mind, chalking it up to an injured woman in pain who needed medical assistance.

Finally reaching the top of the stairs after what felt like an eternity of climbing, she turned the corner and entered the master bedroom to see Samantha bound to the bed. Between the leather cuffs and slinky nightgown, Celine stopped dead in her tracks, startled and embarrassed at the intimate position she found her neighbor in.

The surprise must have shown on her face, because again Samantha said, "Please hurry. We have to get out of here."

Snapping out of her trance, Celine moved closer to the bed and worked at the cuff. The leather brace fit tightly around Samantha's wrist, causing Celine to struggle undoing the clasp. Her arthritic fingers prevented her from releasing the strap.

A string of questions came out of Celine's mouth as she continued to fiddle with the buckle. "What happened? Did your husband leave you like this? Is he home? Are you hurt?"

"No, please just hurry, he'll be back soon," Samantha croaked, frustrated with the old lady's pace.

Just as she began to make progress undoing the first restraint, she noticed a change in Samantha's demeanor. The bound woman took on a solemn expression and the color drained from her face. Celine saw Samantha's eyes go wide with shock, drawing her focus away from the buckle. Concerned with the look of dismay on Samantha's horrified face, she began, "What's wro..."

Celine's voice cut out before she could finish the question. It was replaced by a metallic thud and followed by a deep ringing sound. The vibrations from the aluminum bat connecting with the side of her head sounded like a tuning fork. The impact to Celine's cranium instantly shattered her skull, sending fragments of bone deep into her brain matter. Her body crumpled from the blow, falling to a rest on the bed. The old woman's head flopped onto Samantha's chest, knocking the wind out of her. Samantha's diaphragm began moving up and down rapidly with each breath, hyperventilating with fear from the sudden turn of events. Celine lay still, bent over the bed with her head resting on Samantha's chest. It looked as if she was listening to the bound woman's heartbeat.

The undulating motion of Samantha's chest as she gasped for breath caused the old woman to slide off the bed in a comically slow fashion, leaving a trail of blood in her path before landing on the carpet with a soft thud.

Chandler stood at the foot of the bed with the metal instrument gripped tightly in both hands. Samantha recognized her husband's bat, which had seen plenty of use in his first responder baseball league but doubled as a means of protection for the family in case of a home invader. Of course, they'd never needed it for self-defense until now.

"Well, this is an unfortunate turn of events. I had hoped to avoid any more violence," he said. Looking down at the unconscious, or possibly dead, woman's body before saying, "You've always been a nosy neighbor. Maybe this will teach you to mind your business."

The shock of seeing such brutality mere inches from her face left Samantha speechless. She felt wet droplets of blood dripping down her forehead that had sprayed her from the blow. The room was silent except for the sound of her labored breathing. Her lungs shuddered for air. Taking quick, sharp breaths in and out through her mouth only exacerbated her dry throat.

Samantha watched as Chandler paced back and forth in front of the bed. Mumbling under his breath, he was clearly distraught over attacking the old lady.

The crunching sound echoed in Samantha's head as she replayed the bat's impact against the poor woman's skull. The blow's force could have been enough to kill, and Samantha doubted someone Celine's age could recover from such an injury.

Chandler glanced back up at her with a look of sadness. "Babe. What's going on? You knew I was coming right back so we could have a chat. Why was she here? I really wish you didn't have to see that. I feel like we were making some good progress this morning, but I hope this doesn't change your impression of me. I'm not a bad guy, but I'll do anything to protect my family."

Samantha didn't reply. She couldn't reply. Even if she had the words, her brain didn't know how to translate them into sounds. She could only lay there and stare at him in a state of terror.

A moan escaped from Celine's lips, breaking the silence. Apparently, the blow hadn't killed her. Chandler leaned the bat against the wall and bent down to check on the injured woman. Chandler didn't want her to die, but he couldn't allow her to go either. Leaving her on the floor as a reminder of his brazen act would be detrimental to winning over Samantha.

Looking at his love, he said, "Don't worry. She's going to be okay. I'm just going to bring her downstairs where she'll be more comfortable."

Beginning to calm down but still sniffling heavily from the ordeal, Samantha said, "P-Please. W-Water."

Chandler's realization that he failed to provide a drink for his captive wife dawned on him and he replied, "Oh my god, I’m so sorry. I didn't even think about that. You must be parched. I’ll be right back in a minute.”

The man picked up Celine’s feet and dragged the unconscious woman across the floor and through the bedroom door. A tear ran down Samantha’s cheek while she listened to the dull thud of the old woman’s head hitting each step as Chandler dragged her down the stairs.

Chapter Eighteen

CHANDLER RETURNED TO THE bedroom five minutes later holding a large glass of water. A straw, complete with flexible neck, drifted between the ice cubes clinking inside the cup as he walked across the room. As soon as he saw his captive love, his eyes lit up, leaving any concern for his injured neighbor at the door. The smile that spread across his face showed the genuine joy he felt whenever he gazed upon his wife's beauty. He approached the bed casually, as if he didn't just drag a critically injured woman out of the room only minutes before.

"Here, hon. I'm so sorry about the water. It completely slipped my mind. If you said something earlier, I would have been happy to get some for you."

Giving no reply, Samantha eagerly accepted the straw and closed her lips around the tube. She drained half the glass before coming up for air. Instant relief washed over her parched throat, and the cold sensation of the water in her belly slowly spread as she felt the liquid working its way through her body.

In that moment of silence, with her eyes closed and enjoying the refreshment, Chandler wasn't standing over her holding the glass and there were no restraints tying her to the bed. For a split second, her arms didn't ache from holding an outstretched position all night, and her bladder didn't feel ready to burst from lack of relief.

These were the last seconds of peace while she considered her options. Instinct told her to scream, but she tried that already. She had the urge to flail her body in anger at being held against her will. She wanted to tell Chandler that he had lost his fucking mind, that if he had even a shred of decency, he would release her immediately.

Unfortunately, she didn't think she'd get very far with that attitude considering the lengths Chandler had gone to feed his delusion. He hadn't come this far simply to release her and go back home. No, she had to give him what he wanted–a family complete with a doting and obedient wife.

"Thanks, Chandler," she said. "I understand you've been through a lot but....,"

"It's Kevin."

"What?" she asked.

"My name is Kevin. You called me Chandler. Isn't that the neighbor?" he replied.

Samantha didn't know how to respond. *Is he so far gone that he doesn't even know who he is anymore?* The man was clearly off his rocker, and she didn't know what to make of his claim. He really believed he was her husband. It made no sense to her. He must be having some sort of mental break, but she was no psychologist and had no interest in diagnosing the lunatic. She reminded herself to just play along, and, eventually, he would let his guard down.

"Oh right. My mistake, Kevin," she said, then added, "Thank you for the water. Can you untie me so I can go to the bathroom now?"

Chandler sighed. "Unfortunately, I'm not sure we're at that stage in our relationship yet–especially after that little incident while I was out. But don't worry. I have just the thing. I'll be back in a minute."

He disappeared out of the bedroom, leaving Samantha alone again. Chandler made his way to the backyard and around the fence, over to his old property. Going through the motions as if on autopilot, he no longer bothered to reconcile his mental jumps back and forth between houses and personas. He would be whoever he needed to be at that moment.

Entering the house, he made a quick trip inside to pick up a few items. He liked the convenience of having his old life and things available but knew the risk he took by going back there. He realized settling into his new life right next door could be a problem, but he couldn't worry about that for now. He had to make Samantha see the truth about their destiny together. Then they could leave this town behind and find a new place to settle down together. After only a minute inside, he headed back next door, and just as quickly as he left, he slipped back into his new identity, ready to tend to Samantha's every need.

Samantha heard the back door close and had an idea where Chandler went based on her request, but her fears were realized when he entered holding the small, metal bedpan in his hand.

"See?" he said with a happy, loving smile that seemed to be plastered on his face anytime Samantha saw him. "I got you covered."

"You want me to pee in there? That's disgusting."

"It's really not that bad," he replied. "Have you ever used one before? Especially since your legs are free. It should be a piece of cake. I'll help..."

"I don't need any help," she replied bitterly, cutting him off.

"No, no. I didn't mean that. I'll give you your privacy. I just meant I would help you get in position and... uhh. Well, I have to take off your underpants. But don't worry! This is purely clinical. I'm used to helping my...," he cut himself off this time as his brain short circuited, fighting to come to terms with his new guise while remembering his mother. Finally, instead of giving it any more thought, he continued with the generic. "I've used them before." His tone lost much of its confidence, sounding apprehensive and more like a question than a statement.

Bringing the bedpan over to Samantha, he picked up a towel from a pile of laundry and said, "Lift up. You know, just in case you spill a few drops. See, I've done this before, I'm a professional, no worries," he said with a wink.

The discomfort of her bladder nagged at her and with an offer of relief, she begrudgingly obliged, regardless of the indignity of it all. Supporting herself with shoulders and feet, she lifted her body up while Chandler slid the towel underneath her raised buttocks. The awkward position looked as if she were performing an advanced yoga position or something out of the *Kama Sutra*. With her pelvis held high in the air, Chandler lifted her nightgown to expose her cotton panties and took hold of the waistband at her hips.

Samantha considered kicking him in the face. Their positions gave her the perfect shot. A good blow could knock him unconscious if she got lucky, but what would that accomplish? Even if she killed him, she'd still be tied to the bed. She had to remain patient.

Instead, she held her position and suppressed her emotions while Chandler gently slid her underpants down along her thighs. She shivered as his fingers traced along her legs and down past her knees before slipping them off her feet.

To Samantha's surprise, Chandler did as promised, with no impropriety, although he couldn't help the pressure building in his pants as his hand glided along the supple skin of her legs.

Ignoring his growing urges, Chandler put the bedpan underneath her raised butt and turned to leave the room. In place of the bedpan he entered with, he now held her freshly removed underpants. When Samantha saw the pattern, she realized they were the same ones she had been wearing yesterday before Chandler entered her house and her life. Maybe he was being truthful with her after all. He closed the door, giving her the privacy he promised, leaving her mind etched with the image of him standing in the hall holding her panties up to his face.

Chapter Nineteen

Relieving herself in the bedpan with her bare cheeks resting on the cold metal, Samantha wondered what she did to deserve this. She was a loving mother who tried her best to keep her husband happy regardless of his haughty demeanor. She knew she should have left him years ago, if not for her sake then for the benefit of Dylan. Still, she didn't think playing the part of the subservient wife to a fault warranted the punishment she now received.

Unable to sit up properly, the process was more difficult than Chandler had made it out to be. After posturing herself into what she thought was the ideal position, she released her bladder and a powerful stream gushed into the pan, sending a shudder of relief through her body. The stream's force caused a spray of urine to leap back out of the pan with every squirt, splattering her legs with the warm liquid. Although the container collected a large amount of the pee, by the time she was done her lower half was wet enough that she felt she should have relieved herself in the bed hours ago.

As soon as she finished, a slight tap on the door caused it to open just enough for Chandler to peek his head inside. "All done?" he asked. After seeing the wet towel and legs he added, "Well, I guess you could have used a little help after all. Don't worry, it's nothing to be embarrassed about."

Samantha glared at him but remained silent, her humiliation turning into anger. She had no interest in giving him the satisfaction of a reply. Instead, she turned her gaze to the ceiling, staring through the wall at a far-off spot in the distance. She felt her emotions bubbling up inside of her but willed herself to remain calm and silent.

Years of a bad marriage that included arguments almost every night, which often turned physical, gave Samantha a hardened outer shell. She had plenty of practice creating a secret room in her mind, blocking out the actions around her and keeping her feelings bottled up. Her situation now was hardly different from what she had been living with for so long. The funny part was, when Chandler said he'd never hurt her, she believed him more than when Kevin used to say it to her. Maybe it was because she'd been through so many broken promises and matching bruises with Kevin but also because, regardless of his disturbing actions and unhinged thoughts, she believed Chandler really loved her in a way that Kevin never did.

While Sam was lost in her thoughts, Chandler removed the bedpan and towel, replacing the towel with a fresh one from the closet. He returned with a bowl of warm water and a washcloth.

"Now, let's see if we can't get you cleaned up a little," he said.

He dipped the cloth in the water and wrung it out before wiping it slowly across her forehead. The balmy fabric sent a shiver of relaxing pleasure throughout her. Seeing no point in fighting the comfort, she closed her eyes and enjoyed the moment of solace. She allowed her mind to drift off to another plane while he cleansed the sweat from her skin, until she found herself floating on the edge of consciousness.

The warming sensation moved about her face in a calming manner as Chandler massaged her temples in gentle circles. He noticed the streak of blood across her chest and nightgown, grimacing at the sight of it. It was a reminder of something he'd prefer to forget. He regretted soiling such beauty with his violent act but reminded himself that he committed those atrocities in the name of protecting his family.

He wiped at the marks, slipping her shoulder strap down her arm to expose the area around the bloodied skin. After a few strokes across her partially exposed chest, he removed most of the blood coating her skin, leaving only a faint pink discoloration where the vital fluid had spilled.

Cleaning the red stain from the fabric of her gown would be another story. The peach-colored material, still soaked through with sweat, turned translucent in the light and Chandler couldn't help himself from admiring her beauty. The way the damp fabric clung to her body, she might as well have been naked in front of him. He wanted to remove the gown and wash it with soap in the sink, but with her being awake, he felt she wouldn't approve of being disrobed. He knew he still had a ways to go before she would be ready for that.

It took every urge he had to restrain himself from having his way with her right then and there. In her current condition, it didn't look like she would put up much of a fight. But he didn't feel right taking advantage of her while she was still under the influence of the drugs he gave her. The water she sucked down earlier had more of the sedative in it, although not nearly as much as she drank the previous night. He needed her to stay lucid for their time together today. He'd wean her off it once they could trust each other completely. He longed for the day that they could truly be themselves around each other. Until then, Chandler would happily play the role of caretaker. He viewed it as no different than caring for his mother in his old life. The only difference was his new patient was a lot more pleasant to be around. And although he didn't feel right touching her in her current state, there was nothing wrong with looking. In fact, close observation of the patient is a hallmark of a good nurse. He considered himself a professional after all.

Chandler dunked the cloth in the bowl of water and squeezed it over Samantha, letting the excess liquid drip onto the soiled section of her nightgown. With his hand holding the material from the inside, he scrubbed at the fabric. He continued to work at the bloody gown but knew his futile efforts would fail to remove the stain. "We should get this into the wash right away, but unfortunately I think it might be ruined. I'm really sorry. I'll be happy to replace it."

Samantha was struggling to focus, so she allowed her mind to continue wandering. Being tied to the bed and half naked, she wondered why he hadn't tried to rape her yet. To her surprise, he continued to work at the tough stain, pulling the dress down as he scrubbed it but ignoring her exposed breast. After a minute, he looked at her and said, "I know what you're thinking. I'll never get it clean if I keep using this bloody washcloth, and you're right."

In truth, she couldn't care less about the nightgown. She was past the point of caring about the blood, or the urine either. They seemed like problems from another life that no longer mattered. She wanted to tell him to leave it, to keep massaging her temples with the warm cloth, but her head swayed in a daze. If not for the pillow supporting it, she wondered if her head might roll off to the floor, spinning helplessly away from the rest of her body. She opened her mouth to tell him to keep going but she only mumbled a few unintelligible sounds. Only she understood her words as the medicine worked its way through her body. She knew her tranquil reaction was out of the ordinary for her situation, but she possessed no will for anything other than to lay there and rest. She felt as if she was laying on a bed of clouds floating on the breeze.

"Hello. Samantha. Wake up."

The voice pulled her out of the darkness. Her eyes fluttered open as she adjusted to her surroundings. Feeling a trickle of drool creeping down the side of her chin, she couldn't tell if it had been five minutes or five hours since her last coherent thought.

The voice continued, "I'm sure it's getting to be a bit uncomfortable, so I'm going to trust you, and I hope this will prove that you can trust me as well." The words sounded wavy, like a recording being played back at a slower speed. She tried to understand the meaning but the sounds echoed in her head, giving her no hope of deciphering their intent. The voice played over and over in her mind like it was in a foreign language until it became a collection of syllables, losing all meaning.

A form leaned over her. The smell of stale deli meat permeated her nostrils as she felt someone's warm breath on her face. She sensed a face only inches from her own. The person fumbled with something at her wrist, causing the pressure to increase before a sudden relief flowed through her arm. The soft tingling sensation turned into scathing pins and needles running from her fingers to her elbows as her arms dropped beside her to the bed.

With her hands free, she surprised herself by not wanting to pummel her captor repeatedly with them. Even if they didn't feel like appendages made of jello, she had no desire to harm him. She knew her lack of response to the abuse was due to the drugs in her system, but she didn't care. Her attention remained focused on the twisting arms at her sides, which felt more like tentacles writhing in the sea. The dangling appendages slithered at her sides while the blood rushed to restore circulation to the useless extremities. She clenched and released her fists repeatedly as the blood worked its way through her body until her arms regained a semblance of normalcy. Chandler placed a hand on her back and helped her into a sitting position, where she remained for a moment while the spinning room slowed its rotation.

"You still seem quite groggy. I think a warm shower will wake you up. What do you say?"

Before she knew what was happening, she was on her feet. Walking in a daze, Samantha put one foot in front of the other without a second thought as Chandler led her to the bathroom like a puppy following its owner.

Seeing his wife's blank gaze, Chandler knew if he didn't help her she would stare at the wall for an hour. Apparently, he had given her more of the sedative than she needed, but he hoped a shower would help bring her back to reality. He turned the water on and helped Samantha out of her nightgown, releasing the other strap and letting the dress fall to the floor at her feet. Her mind still a blur, she stepped forward into the stream of warm water making no facial expression, leaving her attention focused on the white tile in front of her.

"Hopefully, this shower will snap you out of your funk. I'll give you some privacy. Give a shout if you need anything. I'll be right outside."

Chapter Twenty

CHANDLER EXITED THE BATHROOM while Samantha freshened up, giving him a moment to look around the bedroom while he waited. With a few minutes alone while Samantha recharged in the shower, Chandler perused the house for any remnants of her previous life that could crack the ideal fantasy world he painstakingly created. He spent hours the previous night, while Samantha slept, getting rid of anything that could remind her of Kevin and the awful memories that came along with him. He wanted to make sure he removed anything that could trigger bad memories or fear for Samantha. She should feel safe in her own home, and he had to eliminate any reminders of her old life

Replacing family photos with carefully edited images, Chandler digitally stitched himself into their joyous memories and celebrations. Pictures of him at Dylan's birthday parties over the years and his wedding to Samantha now adorned the walls and mantles.

He picked up a frame decorated with golden flowers from the nightstand and looked at the portrait within. It showed a happy family of three going for a walk in the park. He never imagined seeing himself with such a beautiful wife and child, living the proverbial American dream. The only thing missing was the white picket fence, which if he was being honest, he could do without. White picket fences weren't very high and allowed neighbors to see right through them. Chandler preferred a brick wall between him and the outside world. He didn't need anything or anyone except his soulmate and son. He smiled at the thought of a world with just the three of them. They could be happy together, forever.

The doorbell broke his concentration, and his face twisted in a grimace at the distraction. "What now?" he said under his breath to the empty room. He picked up the phone, which buzzed along with the doorbell sound, and looked at the image being transmitted from the camera. He still marveled at such a convenient invention. He should have gotten one of these long ago, although every time he looked at the camera through the phone, he worried about pressing the wrong button and allowing the caller to hear or, even worse, see him. He enjoyed the idea of watching from the shadows, just like from his perch at the window.

Opening the app, he saw Dana Summers standing at the front door wearing another gray blazer with matching skirt and a baby blue button-up shirt underneath. The fashionable real estate agent carried a shopping bag in one hand and held a folder in the other.

Why were there so many interruptions? Chandler watched the screen and prayed for her to leave after the doorbell went unanswered but to his dismay, the door creaked open and Dana peeked her head inside.

"Hello? Is anyone home? You left the lockbox open and the key was in the door. You should really be more careful," said Dana as she crossed the threshold into the house, undeterred by the unattended key left in the door.

"Hello?" she repeated, walking further into the living room and entering the kitchen. "It's me, Dana. Is anyone home? I just stopped by to drop off a few things for the open house tomorrow. I've received a lot of interest in the property. I think we'll get at least one offer. If we're lucky we might even have a bidding war and go over the asking price."

Chandler waited halfway up the stairs, holding his breath as Dana looked for a sign that anyone was home. He doubted she needed to go upstairs but was prepared to pounce on her if she did. With any luck, she would put her things on the kitchen table and leave without causing a disturbance.

"Sam? Kevin? Are you guys here? I hope I'm not interrupting anything. If I am, don't mind me. I'll just leave the flyers on the table. I brought some cookies for tomorrow also. The weirdest thing though, did you guys see the police car across the street? I guess your neighbor has gone missing. She activated her emergency bracelet but when they arrived at her house, they couldn't find her anywhere. They're looking around the neighborhood now to see if she wandered off and got hurt or lost. Anyway, I'll let you guys get back to it, I'm sure you don't want to hear me babbling all day."

Still holding his breath in anticipation, praying to avoid another confrontation, Chandler slowly inhaled from his hiding spot on the stairs. He hoped his deliberately slow breath would muffle any sound from escaping his lips. A sigh of relief washed over him when he heard Dana deposit the items on the table and make her way back through the living room towards the front door. Chandler thanked his lucky stars she was about to leave of her own volition but just as she was about to exit the house, he heard a noise. Judging by Dana's sudden stop and head turn, she heard it too.

A long groan came from down the hallway on the first floor. Chandler instantly knew the source of the noise. In his haste to return to Samantha, he dragged the old woman into the nearest room at the bottom of the steps. He hadn't worried about her going anywhere after the blow to the head but in hindsight, he should have finished her off when he had the chance. Apparently, she had regained consciousness long enough to activate her emergency bracelet. Unfortunately for her, but luckily for Chandler, the model she wore didn't include a GPS tracker. Any hope of being found inside the house across the street would be unlikely, but all of these unwanted guests were hampering his fantasy.

Still in and out of consciousness, Celine heard a voice talking far in the distance. She couldn't hear the words but somehow knew her only chance of being saved stood on the other side of the door that loomed over her.

Mustering the rest of her strength, she tried to call for help but instead let out an unintelligible groan. Although no words escaped her lips, she hoped the sound was loud enough to alert the voice's owner that she needed help.

Celine's attempt at gaining Dana's attention worked. The real estate agent instantly turned back towards the hallway, walking tentatively through the house while looking for the source of the noise. She called out again, "Hello? Samantha, is that you? Are you ok?"

As she approached the closed door hiding the injured woman, Chandler felt like he should be the one groaning. He was so close to getting through the intrusion undisturbed but with the old woman's moan, there was no chance of that now. Always trying to do the right thing, his attempt at avoiding any more senseless violence would only bring more pain and suffering into his world. He shook his head as he crept behind Dana and slipped into the kitchen while she investigated the noise.

Again, Dana called in a shaky voice, "Hello?"

The close proximity of the call prompted a response from behind the door. She heard another groan, this one shorter and quieter than the previous. The sound drew Dana towards the room. As her right hand turned the doorknob and pushed it open, her free hand went to her mouth in horror as her jaw dropped at the sight of the battered woman on the floor. A thick pool of blood from the wound on her head seeped along the wooden floor of the makeshift office.

A floorboard creaked behind her and she turned, coming face-to-face with Chandler. Not expecting the man to be so close behind her, she jumped at the sight of him, letting out a yelp of surprise in the process. She instantly recognized him from their awkward encounter the previous day. "What are you..." she said, but her words cut off as she gasped in shock as Chandler slid a carving knife into her belly.

Dana's eyes immediately glossed over as she looked down at the knife sticking out of her abdomen. Trying to process the situation, she stood there silently, staring at the blade and the hand that held it. After what felt like an eternity of silence, Chandler placed his free hand on her shoulder and gently withdrew the blade from her stomach. Coated in blood, droplets of the red liquid rolled down the edge of the knife and fell to the floor. Her gaze transfixed on the straight incision in her shirt, she watched as the blue fabric hatched a dark purple stain. The wet discoloration grew rapidly in size as the blood gushed from the wound.

She didn't feel any pain except for a small pinch in her tummy but upon seeing the copious amount of blood spill from her stomach, reality hit Dana suddenly and her lungs let loose a series of loud screams as she backed away from her assailant. Her hands instinctively went to her stomach, putting pressure on the wound. As she retreated, she tripped on Celine and tumbled backwards, sprawling on top of the injured woman lying helpless on the floor behind her.

With Dana still screaming while she tried to make sense of the situation, Chandler fell on top of her, plunging the knife into her chest again and attempting to cover her mouth to stifle her cries. Their faces were only inches from each other, sharing the same panicked look, albeit for different reasons. He pleaded with her to be quiet as his blade continued to slice into her chest, sending blood flying through the air.

In a final desperate attempt to save herself, Dana put her hand up towards Chandler's face, aiming to scratch at his eyes, but her wounds had already sucked her strength dry. It looked more like she was feeling her way around a dark cave rather than fending off an attacker.

A final plunge into Dana's neck took the last of her life. Her arms fell down to the ground and her shouts ceased. She lay motionless, still pinned to the floor by Chandler and laid out on top of Celine.

Soaked in the realtor's blood, Chandler struggled as he attempted to stand. He lost his grip and did a face plant into the dead woman's bloody chest, coating himself with the sticky substance.

Finally, he stood up and looked at the mayhem in front of him. The vast amounts of blood splashed about the room didn't even seem real. It looked as if someone poured buckets of fake blood on the floor for a B horror movie. Apparently, in his wild attacks, an errant blow from the knife sliced open Celine's neck as she lay prone beneath the scuffle. Her open artery quickly sapped her last hold on life, killing the old woman. It was just as well. Even with years of rehab, she would never fully recover from her injuries, nevermind the jeopardy she put his family in just by being alive. The cops were outside looking for her right now. The real estate agent was dead because of her. As a lifelong family friend, he understood putting her down to be the correct course of action. It was a mercy killing for her and one less loose end for him to worry about. The real estate agent on the other hand... well, she just happened to be in the wrong place at the wrong time. It was a shame, but his hands were tied.

Chapter Twenty-One

BETWEEN THE SOUND OF the shower and the bathroom fan, Samantha heard nothing of the commotion happening downstairs. Even if the sounds of two women being brutally murdered below her feet made it through the walls, she might not have cared enough to do anything about it.

The feeling of the hot water's steady stream pounding in a repeating pattern against her skin lulled her senses. She closed her eyes and swayed in the waterfall while she imagined receiving a full body treatment in a spa at a tropical resort. The shower had awoken her from her drugged out stupor but after a minute alone in the relaxing cascade, her mind drifted and any thoughts of Chandler or her situation had become lost to the tingling sensation of the warm water massaging her body.

She could have stood there in a daze for hours, basking in the warmth while her aching muscles recovered their stamina. Her mental paralysis was so complete she didn't even notice the shower door opening and Chandler joining her in the wash.

The water at their feet instantly turned pink as the spray washed the blood from his body. As the high pressure shower head swept the fresh blood away, more ran down his legs to replace it. Chandler lathered a bar of soap and scrubbed along his arms and face, attempting to remove any remaining residue from his skin.

Samantha lingered in bewilderment. The colored water hypnotized her as it swirled in the shower basin. She watched the sudsy pink liquid trickle between her toes before disappearing down the drain.

Minutes ticked away as Chandler continued to scour his body, removing the last of the pink stains. His furious scrubbing irritated his skin, turning the flesh as red as the stubborn stain.

The two stood next to each other in silence. The only interaction between the pair was their bare hips bumping into each other as they vied for the water's warm embrace.

Suddenly, cold air rushed around Samantha, causing her body to shiver with goosebumps. The abrupt change in temperature woke her up from the trance, snapping her back to reality. The water had stopped and Chandler released the knob, cutting off the source of the warmth.

"Babe, how are you feeling? We have to get ready to go."

The words surprised Samantha. She looked at Chandler with confusion on her face. "Go?" she asked.

"Yeah," Chandler replied as he pushed her hair out of her eyes and tucked it behind her ear. "I thought we could make it work here, but I've realized it's not possible. There's just too many distractions. But don't worry... I have the perfect place for us to get away. We'll be all alone and won't have to worry about any more interruptions."

"Interruptions?" she parroted back to him, barely coherent enough to understand who she was talking to, much less the meaning of his words.

"Don't worry about it," he replied. "Just get dressed and pack a small bag. We'll pick up Dylan on the way."

"Dylan," she repeated, the effects of the drugs still heavily affecting her cognitive state. The suggestion of going to see Dylan was the first thing she understood from the conversation. "That sounds good," she mumbled.

Stepping out of the shower, Chandler grabbed a towel from the small linen closet in the corner and held it out, offering it to Samantha. She looked at the towel but made no move to accept it. Her mind had already drifted back to a dissociative state.

Noticing the blank stare on Samantha's face, Chandler wrapped the towel around her, rubbing her shoulders to help her dry off. Apparently, the preparations for their trip relied solely on him. He was happy to oblige, but the police across the street searching for their missing neighbor was a major cause for concern. They had to leave as soon as possible and needed to do it without raising suspicion.

Chandler continued to dry Samantha's body, taking a moment to appreciate her curves as he caressed her with the towel. He felt the blood rush to his groin, sending his hormones into overdrive as he admired her. Proud of himself at showing restraint so far, he didn't know how much longer he could contain himself. Standing naked next to such beauty, he needed a release. Although tempted to have his way with her the previous night while she was unconscious, he didn't believe in taking advantage of her like that. He needed her to be a willing participant and was confident they would reach that level in their relationship with a bit of patience.

With Samantha mostly dry, he wrapped the towel around her waist and tucked the flap in by her hip. Bringing his hand up to her face, he touched her cheek with the backside of his index finger. Every time he made contact with her, the softness of her skin surprised him. He traced a line down her neck to her shoulder, running along the edge of her protruding collarbone. From there he followed the curve of her armpit down the side of her chest. He inhaled deeply as he cupped her exposed breast, circling his finger around her nipple. Delicately squeezing the supple flesh, he felt her whole body quiver under his touch. Not knowing if her shiver was from the warmth of his hand or a shudder of revulsion, he could only hope it was the former. She remained still, making no reaction to his touch other than the involuntary shudder. He took it as a good sign that she made no move to stop him.

He knew they didn't have time for delays, but he felt like he could explode at any moment. With a real woman standing in front of him, he couldn't pass up the opportunity. He moved his hand down her side slowly from her breast to her hip, sliding under the towel and allowing it to fall to the floor. Putting his arm around her, he drew her in close, allowing the contours of their bodies to merge as one. Chandler brushed his lips against her neck and drew air in deeply through his nose, inhaling the scent of her freshly showered body. He grabbed hold of her butt and pulled their bodies together even tighter. Within a few moments of their embrace, he could no longer contain himself, nor did he want to, and allowed himself to climax, spilling his seed onto the shower floor. After he finished, without a thought he whispered the words, "I love you." Standing together, holding the love of his life in his arms felt like pure heaven to Chandler.

Strangely enough, for a brief moment, Samantha had a feeling of security, too. He was gentle with her in a way she hadn't experienced in a long time. Regardless of the drug's lingering effects, she knew that in his own weird way Chandler did love her and would never hurt her. Not willingly, at least. That's not something she could say for Kevin. In truth, Chandler helped her out of a bad relationship that she never would have ended on her own. The problem was, while saving her from one bad relationship, he forced her into another without her consent. Still, she couldn't shake the feeling that she was better off than before. She knew her thoughts were irrational, but she couldn't help her feelings. She wanted to scream but found she had no energy to do so.

Instead, she did what she always did after getting out of the shower. She followed her usual routine like muscle memory, although a little slower than usual, and went to her closet to get dressed.

Chandler moved at a much quicker pace, dressing himself and grabbing a few outfits at random from Kevin's closet. After packing his bag, he went to the window to survey the activity on the street. Looking outside, he half expected to see a police helicopter and SWAT team closing in on him. What used to be his favorite pastime, peacefully looking out his window at the people in his neighborhood, now filled him with fear and anxiety as he peered through the shades.

As the real estate agent mentioned, a single police car was parked in the driveway across the street. Chandler didn't see the officer anywhere but knew they wouldn't be far. Contemplating the logistics of getting to the car undetected, timing would be everything. Chandler had plenty of experience playing this game. Based on the way things have been going for him, he knew luck would be in his favor. He had an idea how they could escape undetected.

He went back to the bedroom to find Samantha dressed but spacing out again, having failed to pack any clothes. He grabbed a few things for her and said, "Listen, I know this isn't an ideal situation, but we can't let anyone see you in this condition." He took hold of her hand and massaged it, as if consoling a close friend. "No offense, you just look a little out of it. Anyway, you're going to need some more medicine so you can sleep in the back for the ride."

Samantha watched him pour a cloudy white liquid from a brown bottle into a small, clear medicine cup.

"I need you to drink this," he said as if speaking to a child. He put the cup filled with the powerful sedative to her lips. Offering no resistance, Samantha's mouth opened slightly, and she accepted the medicine inside, swallowing it down in two gulps.

Chandler placed the cup back on the table and wiped the excess medicine from her lips with his thumb. After licking his finger, he went to the storage closet and retrieved Kevin's large suitcase. He undid the zipper and opened the flap of the bag.

"It might actually be a little easier if you get in on your own," he said.

Samantha stared at the open suitcase and frowned, shaking her head slightly from side to side. "I don't want to go in there," she murmured.

Chandler sighed. "I'm really sorry, but there's no other way. It won't be for long, I promise," he replied, hoping to soothe her fears. "How about this? I won't close it all the way. You'll be fine." Even with his words of encouragement, he saw the fear in her sad eyes, something he hoped was behind them at that point. He wanted to see her happy and full of joy, not in this pathetic state.

"Please, don't make me."

He turned away, taking a few strides across the living room, and punched himself twice in the side of the head. Grumbling in an agitated tone he said, "Damn it, I knew I should have just waited until after she fell asleep." Furious at himself for upsetting her, he knew he'd have to make the best of it.

Turning back to Samantha, he saw a broken woman. Her hunched back and sullen face gave her a look of defeat. Chandler hated seeing her this way but knew it would all be over soon. Samantha's legs wobbled, and he put his arms around her, keeping her steady as the drug worked its way through her body.

"Relax, you can wait here with me a minute. I'm sorry about all the medicine, but I think it helped us make a lot of progress in a short period. I mean... look at us," he said as she pushed her chin up gently, causing their eyes to meet. He held her for a minute, enjoying the calm before the storm, until her forehead came to a rest on his chest and she began a soft snore in his arms.

Lowering her body to the ground, she fit snugly into the suitcase. Positioning her inside had been easier than Chandler expected. After a few false starts and twisted limbs, he came to realize putting her upper body in first with her back along the side of the bag left plenty of room to tuck her legs up to her chest. From there he closed the zipper around her quite easily.

He looked out the window one last time to ensure the street remained clear before heading to the car with the two smaller bags first, throwing them in the backseat. From this new vantage point, he scanned the road again and saw no sign of the officer whose car sat across the street.

He hurried back inside to get the large suitcase containing Samantha. As he rolled the suitcase down the walkway towards the car, Chandler was thankful he didn't have to carry it the entire distance. He imagined the spectacle that would create.

He wheeled it down the path as quickly as possible while being extra careful with the precious cargo. The unconscious woman inside made no objection when the bag dropped two steps along the walkway to the car. Chandler pressed the trunk button on the key and came to a stop behind the car. Taking one last glance down the street and seeing no one in sight, he crouched next to the bag and prepared himself to lift the heavy load.

With a small grunt, he picked up the bag and placed it squarely inside the trunk. Once safely inside, he opened the zipper slightly as promised, just enough to give her some extra air, and closed the trunk lid.

No sooner did the sound of the trunk click closed than a voice came from behind him. "Excuse me sir. Are you coming from the Reed residence?"

Startled by the unexpected company, Chandler spun around to find a young officer standing behind him. The cop seemed to come out of nowhere. The officer must have just graduated from the academy, barely looking a day over eighteen years old.

"Sorry, I didn't mean to startle you," he said. "Officer Roberts. I'm here looking for a missing woman. She probably wandered off down the street and got herself lost. Anyway, I was just wondering if Kevin was doing okay since he called out sick today."

Chandler's mind spun. He didn't know what to say. One wrong word here and the jig was up. He could feel his whole plan about to unravel. A bead of sweat rolled down the side of his face. He considered lunging at the officer in an attempt to overpower him but thought better of it. Although short, the man looked spry and with even minimal defense training would have no trouble getting the upper hand over the out-of-shape Chandler.

Instead, Chandler said, "I... ummm. Well, I don't want to get him in trouble."

The cops face scrunched with his expression making a sudden change from jovial to serious. "Hmmm? What do you mean?" he asked.

"Well, he took the missus on a little, romantic getaway. You know, just a couple days in the woods to escape the world. They asked me to stop by and water their plants."

A more experienced officer might have picked up on the waver in his voice or the anxious look in his eyes. Even the sweat running down Chandler's face on an unseasonably cool day should have given him away. Instead, a sudden look of realization came over the cop and his expression relaxed. "Ohhhhh. I get ya. He's playin' hookey. Don't worry, his secret is safe with me. I won't mention it."

"Thanks, I'm sure he'll appreciate it," Chandler replied and turned to get in the car. A smile crept across his face as soon as he had his back to the officer. Another close call but a clean getaway. Chandler felt invincible.

Just as he stepped inside the car, the officer called back to him, "What about the kid?"

"Huh?"

"He has a boy right? You said they went on a romantic getaway," asked Officer Roberts.

"Oh. Uhhh, I....I think he's with his grandparents."

"Ahhh, makes sense. Anyway, if you happen to see an old lady wandering around, give us a holler. Her name is Celine Foster."

Chandler nodded, "Will do. Good luck."

He closed the car door and started the engine. Using the sleeve of his shirt, Chandler wiped the moisture that had accumulated on his forehead. Adjusting the rear view mirror to find the cop, he spotted the man standing across the street on Celine's lawn. The officer stood watching Chandler intently and waited for him to drive away.

Almost home free, Chandler put the car in reverse and allowed it to roll backwards. As he stepped on the gas, he considered pressing his foot down on the accelerator and letting the vehicle plow right into the ignorant officer. Chandler could almost hear the sound of the cop's bones crunching under the tires as he ran over the man. For a second, his urge to do just that almost succeeded but then he remembered his priority. His family. Instead, he allowed the car to turn and roll slowly down the residential street, giving a nod to the officer as he went to pick up his boy from daycare.

Chapter Twenty-Two

CHANDLER HAD MIXED EMOTIONS about leaving his neighborhood behind. In his heart, he knew he'd never be able to return to the street he grew up on or see the familiar faces he watched pass by his window every morning. On the other hand, he had a family now and although his wife currently rode inside a suitcase in the trunk, he imagined a day in the not too distant future where she could sit in the passenger seat beside him. Until then, he would do whatever it took to keep his family safe and together.

The first order of business in keeping the family together was picking up Dylan from daycare. He pulled into the parking lot, already getting used to the routine on only his second trip to the center. He exited the car and fought the urge to check on his companion. A few other parents lingered in the lot and he couldn't risk one of them seeing inside the open trunk.

Instead, he headed towards the school, hoping to be in and out quickly so they could be on their way. Upon entering the building, a receptionist greeted him. She sat at the desk in the entryway, which sat empty earlier that morning. The young brunette, probably in her mid-twenties, looked up from the book that held her attention and gave him a smile.

He nodded and said hello, but as he attempted to pass, she held up a hand and said, "Excuse me, sir. I'm sorry, but I haven't seen you before. Can you tell me who you are here to pick up?"

"Oh, hi," said Chandler, caught off-guard by the question. "Uhhh, I'm here to pick up Dylan Reed."

She smiled at him and said, "Oh, sure. Can I see your ID please? I just need to make sure you're on the list."

"The list?"

The girl rolled her eyes, eager to get back to reading. "The list of approved people for pickups," she replied, annoyed at the question she assumed should have been obvious to him.

"Oh. Well, I'm not sure if I'm on the list. The Reeds went out of town. I didn't think it would be a problem since I dropped Dylan off this morning."

The girl scrunched her face as she considered the statement. "Well, pickups are different from drop offs. We have to follow procedure with who we allow the children to leave with. I'm sure you understand. If you're not on the list, we could give the Reeds a ring to confirm."

"Hmmm, they're on a little getaway and I don't think they have service where they are, but you can try."

Pressing a few keys to bring up the Reed's contact info on her computer, the young lady dialed Samantha's number first. After several rings, the call went to voicemail, as Chandler knew it would.

With a frustrated look on her face, she pressed the receiver on the phone while keeping the handset to her ear. After a moment, she released it and dialed the number for Kevin. To both of their surprise, the phone in Chandler's back pocket rang.

Chandler took the device from his pants and answered the call, looking at the receptionist while he spoke into the phone. "Hello, Mr. Reed's phone," he said into the receiver while keeping eye contact with the girl. "I completely forgot. He gave me his phone in case anything came up. You know, with Dylan or something."

"He *gave* you his phone?" she asked incredulously, not understanding why someone would just hand over their phone on their way out of town for a long weekend.

"Yeah, well, you know. Us old folks, we don't have our whole lives on there like you kids do," he said, and then quickly added, "Plus, I'm pretty sure he has another phone for work."

"Ohhhhhhhh," she replied, starting to understand but still seeming skeptical. "Well, I'm going to need some sort of approval. You'll have to hold on for a few minutes. You can have a seat over there." She motioned to a few folding chairs against the wall behind him.

Who the hell did this girl think she is, keeping him from seeing his own child. Chandler felt like jumping over the desk and beating her to a pulp. She'd regret asserting her authority rather quickly with his hands around her throat.

Their eyes remained locked for an awkward moment as he considered her command. He hoped she didn't see the fire in his eyes, but he had a hard time suppressing his anger. The sound of the door opening behind him broke their gaze. A pair of mothers walked in and prevented Chandler from taking any drastic action.

The girl behind the desk smiled at the newcomers and waved them in. The ease at which the other parents could pick up their children made Chandler's rage return even more fiercely than before. *Why could they waltz right through when he had to jump through hoops to get Dylan?*

Luckily for Chandler, his brains came out on top of his emotions, and he took a seat to wait while the young woman behind the desk went into the classroom. What would he do if they didn't let Dylan leave with him? He couldn't walk out of there without the boy. They needed to hit the road before the police started looking for him. Chandler could feel the walls closing in on him with every moment that ticked by, but he took a breath to calm himself and stave off the looming panic attack.

A stream of parents came and went while Chandler waited for the receptionist's return. Finally, after a long delay, she came back with another woman, most likely Dylan's teacher. The boy trailed behind the two ladies and squealed with glee when he saw Chandler.

"You're here for Dylan?" the teacher asked, noticing the boy's delight.

Chandler tried to remember if it was the same woman from the morning drop off, but he kept his head down earlier to avoid eye contact. "Yes, his parents are away, so I'm watching him. I'm sort of like an unofficial uncle," said Chandler, putting on the friendliest smile he could muster.

"Well, we're not supposed to do this, but I did notice you brought him in this morning and he clearly knows you," his teacher said, glancing at the boy. "Plus, I can't sit around all night if no one else is coming to get him."

"Great! Thanks, I really appreciate it. I'm sorry I'm not on the list or whatever it is. It's probably because I'm from out of town, so I'm not usually available. You know, in case of an emergency or anything," he explained.

"Okay, well, make sure to tell the Reeds to call us and get you added right away," she said.

"No problem, I will tell them. Thanks again," he said as he put his hand on the boy's shoulder and they turned to walk out the door.

Outside, Chandler barely contained his giddiness. What almost turned into a catastrophe ended up working out fine. Keeping a cool head and waiting for a beneficial outcome was surely the correct choice. He thought of the saying *cooler heads will prevail.* It was a mantra he needed to keep reminding himself of to prevent any more unwanted confrontations.

As they approached the car, he asked the boy, "Hey, do you like camping?"

The boy's face lit up. "I've never been camping before. I always wanted to go, but Dad told me I wasn't old enough."

“Pssshhhh, that’s poppycock!” Chandler said, ignoring the boy's mention of his other dad. He knew the kid couldn’t be blamed for being confused about the situation. Chandler had a hard time keeping it straight, himself. “We’re going to go on an adventure.”

“What about Mom?” the boy asked.

“Oh, don’t worry. She’s coming too. I wouldn’t dream of going anywhere without her... without either of you.”

Chapter Twenty-Three

SAMANTHA WOKE UP WITH a start from a horrible nightmare. Her eyes jumped open, and she found herself staring at an unfamiliar ceiling. Struggling to make sense of her surroundings, she wondered for a second if the dream could have been real. Paralyzed by fear, she wanted to close her eyes and go back to sleep, but it felt like her eyelids had been glued open. She raised her arms hesitantly and looked at her hands. There were no ropes or handcuffs restricting her movement. The bed she lay on, an old mattress with a small metal frame, didn't even have bedposts. Maybe her nightmare was just that and nothing more than a dream. But then why was she waking up in an unfamiliar location? No, her nightmares were real.

She looked around the room for her captor, but she seemed to be alone. As her eyes came into focus and she inspected the room, she had no recognition of her surroundings. Remaining quiet to listen for anyone else in the vicinity, the house sounded empty other than her. From outside, she heard a cacophony of birds chirping away as they went about their morning but nothing else.

After a long night's rest, the cloud over her mind had cleared. She had no doubts about her dangerous predicament and the need to escape and find the police. She sat up in bed, causing the old springs to make a rusty squeaking sound as she raised her body to a sitting position. The mattress, which was barely more than a portable cot, gave little to no support for her aching body, but considering the other recent positions she'd found herself in, this one seemed a welcome relief. The lingering aches from her bumps and bruises drowned out any back pain from sleeping on the old bed.

The bare room was empty except for the bed and an ancient dresser with a missing drawer in the corner. Constructed from unfinished logs, the wooden walls in the small bedroom allowed cracks of morning sunlight in through the joints in the beams.

Samantha's mind raced with anxiety as she tried to piece together her memories and determine how much of her nightmare had been real. She looked at her wrists and saw bruising from her ordeal the previous day and realized she was in trouble. With her mind clearing and her wits slowly returning, she knew she had to get as far away from this place as fast as possible.

She stood up quickly, maybe a bit too quickly, and a sudden rush of blood to her head caused a wave of dizziness to overtake her. She sat back down for a moment, allowing the head-rush to run its course. Taking a few deep breaths, she stood again, this time steadying herself on the bed as she rose. After testing her balance, she tentatively walked across the room.

She opened the bedroom door and entered the main living area of a small cabin. It looked like a run-down version of a classic hunting cabin, complete with mounted deer heads on the walls and a chandelier constructed from antlers. A stone hearth radiated warmth from a pile of glowing embers that remained in the fireplace. It looked like it had been burning a while. She wondered how long she'd been in this place. She seemed to be alone in the cabin, but her captor couldn't be far. Remaining as quiet as possible, she crept across the main area of the room.

Gaining confidence that she was indeed alone, Samantha moved from window to window, examining the area around the cabin and looking for any signs of life. To her dismay, she saw the same scene outside every window. A small, grassy clearing around the cabin quickly changed into a forest. The dense assortment of trees blocked any view beyond the yard.

Outside one window, however, she saw something that caught her attention. Her green Subaru sat parked in the dirt driveway just outside the house. She needed to find the keys. She had to find them quickly before Chandler returned. The car was her best chance of escape and making it back to civilization for help. With no idea of her location, running through the woods would be a risky endeavor. Maybe she'd find help in a nearby cabin, but more than likely she'd end up lost in the woods with nothing to eat or drink. Even if she followed the road, she didn't know how far she'd have to go until finding help.

Her fears of being unable to find the keys were quickly allayed because after a quick glance around the sparsely furnished cabin, she noticed her keychain hanging on a hook near the kitchen counter. She smiled at her luck and grabbed the keys. Without bothering to put her shoes on, which sat neatly placed by the front door, she made a run for the car. Her only thoughts were to escape and get back to civilization.

Dashing through the dirt in her bare feet, Samantha's legs were still unsteady and her mind disoriented; she stumbled on the way to the car but recovered and made it to the vehicle unscathed. She opened the door and sat in the familiar driver's seat of her own vehicle. A smile widened across her face. It was her first smile in... she didn't know how long. The only thing she cared about was getting away from this place. Freedom was so close; she could taste it.

Taking a moment to compose herself before starting the engine, she saw something emerge from between the trees across the yard. A man. It must be Chandler returning to check on her. She had to move quickly, but she fumbled with the keys as she tried to put them in the ignition. She kept her head down to avoid being seen in the car while peeking above the dash as the figure moved closer.

Finally, after what seemed like an eternity, she heard the click of the key sliding into the ignition. By this time Chandler had traveled half the distance from the woods to the cabin, and she could see his face clearly. About to turn the ignition, she saw something else behind the man and her heart sank. Chandler wasn't alone. Trailing close behind him was another figure. A smaller one. Dylan.

In her disoriented awakening and subsequent hasty escape, she hadn't even considered that her son was here with them. She sank lower in her seat and began to sob, finally letting out the emotions that had been bottled up inside and suppressed by the drugs. Letting the tears roll freely down her cheeks, her hand dropped from the key. She felt her hopes of escape deflate as she slumped down out of view. She couldn't leave now. Not without Dylan.

Chapter Twenty-Four

ON THE DRIVE TO their destination, Chandler told Dylan about all the activities he had planned for them on their camping trip. So when they arrived at the cabin the previous night, Dylan had been excited to start the adventure and explore the surrounding woods immediately. To his dismay, the sun had set by the time they arrived, and Chandler explained to the boy that exploring an unfamiliar forest at night time was asking for trouble. Between wild animals and the chance of getting lost, waiting until morning was the best choice. Plus, he still had to get Samantha out of the trunk and situated in bed to finish sleeping off her meds, hopefully without the boy noticing her travel arrangements. He promised Dylan an early start at first light if he promised to wait until then. Reluctantly, he agreed.

Chandler thought it was best to tell the boy his mother would meet them at the cabin rather than let him see her in such a condition. It pained Chandler to see her that way as well, but now that they had true privacy, there was no need for such measures anymore.

The old hunting cabin had been a favorite spot of Chandler's as a boy. His uncle took him out here every summer. It was his uncle's attempt at filling in the hole left from a lack of a father figure in Chandler's life. He had many fond memories of exploring these woods as a child.

Chandler knew the cabin had been empty for several years, but the state of the building surprised him. In his mind, the cabin still looked exactly the same as his visions of long ago. Vivid pictures of the new memories he was about to make with his family filled his head, but the dilapidated structure needed several major renovations and had water damage from the numerous leaks in the roof. A thick layer of dust coated everything inside the building, leaving the living space less than ideal. Still, those things could be fixed with time and effort. Miles from civilization, this was the perfect spot to start a new life with his family. There would be no visitors and nowhere to run to, although he hoped they were nearing the point where he wouldn't have to worry about Samantha trying to run. Their time together the previous day encouraged him and he felt a closeness to her in a way he's never felt with anyone before.

Once he got the boy to sleep, Chandler unpacked his wife and laid her on the double mattress in the bedroom. Her tangled hair needed brushing and her complexion looked pale due to her cramped quarters on the ride, but she was still beautiful. Chandler laid down in bed next to Samantha, put his arm around her, and gave her a kiss on the cheek. As Chandler drifted off to sleep, he thought about how they could make their home here, for a while at least.

The first one to awake in the morning, Dylan couldn't contain his eagerness to begin the day. Out of bed with the birds at the break of dawn, he barged into the adults' bedroom, hollering for them to get up and get ready. Chandler jumped up at the boy's entrance and quieted the boy's shouts. His mother tossed in bed at the ruckus, mumbled something incomprehensible, and fell back to her slumber.

Chandler touched Samantha's forehead and his palm came away moist with sweat. He said to the boy, "Your mom still needs a few hours to rest, but I know you're really excited to go out. She should be fine here while we have a quick look around."

The child didn't need another invitation. He was out the door before Chandler could even finish getting dressed. By the time Chandler made it outside, the boy was at the tree line looking for anything in the woods that piqued his interest.

It had been years since Chandler's last visit to this place, but he remembered a few landmarks from his childhood. Since they could be staying here for a while, he had plenty of time to refamiliarize himself with the area.

Chandler headed off west from the cabin, whistling at Dylan to gain his attention. "This way," he said to the boy, who immediately took off in the direction of his companion. In only a minute of searching through the overgrowth, Chandler found the remnants of the trail he was looking for.

As they made their way through the woods, he turned to the boy and said, "So, are you ready for a little wilderness survival lesson? If you're lost or stuck in the woods, what's the most important thing to find?"

"Food," replied Dylan confidently.

"Wrong," said Chandler. "Now don't get me wrong, food is important. But the most important thing to find is water. Most people can live without food for over a week, but you can only survive a couple of days without water. So our first task will be to find running water."

After ten minutes of walking while playing games and spotting creatures as they went, Chandler squatted down, put his finger to his lips, and whispered, "Be quiet and listen closely. Ignore the sounds of birds and nearby animals and listen beyond that."

They heard a soft trickling sound of running water in the distance. Following the same direction they had already been walking, the sound grew louder, and after another five minutes, they came to a small creek. The brook flowed nicely, filled with snow runoff from a nearby mountain. Upon coming out of the trees and seeing the water, Dylan ran ahead, hollering with delight.

"Great," said Chandler approvingly. "We completed our mission."

In truth, Chandler knew about the stream in this general direction, but it had been so long since he'd been to this cabin he wasn't sure of the exact location. Luckily it hadn't dried up over the years. He caught up with the boy and bent down next to the water. After washing his hands in the stream, he cupped his hands and brought them to his face, drinking a mouthful of the cold water. Dylan, following the older man's lead, did the same.

"The main reason we were looking for water is to drink, but there's another reason, too," Chandler told the boy. "If you're lost in the woods and you can find running water, following the flow of water downhill will hopefully lead you to civilization."

"But we're not lost, are we?" the boy asked.

"No, no," said Chandler with a laugh. "We're not lost. I'm just trying to teach you about what to do if you ever did get lost. It's a handy skill to have. I used to be a Boy Scout when I was a kid."

"Really?" he asked.

"You bet. Made it all the way to Life Scout. But then I had some problems at school and had to drop out."

"What kind of problems?" the boy asked.

Chandler made a grimace. "I'd rather not get into it. It was a long time ago."

"Well, I want to be a Boy Scout when I get older," Dylan proclaimed.

"That sounds like a great idea," said Chandler. "That reminds me. I have something for you. It's an important tool for every scout to have. But you have to remember to be very careful with it. It's not a toy."

Chandler took out a small wooden object from his pocket. The object had a silver line running along the side. Dylan looked at the tool, unsure of its use but curious about the gift. "What is it?" he asked.

Chandler placed his fingers on a small indentation in the side and pulled a metal blade out on a hinge. "If you're old enough to go exploring in the woods, you're old enough to carry a pocket knife."

The boy's eyes went wide. "A real knife?"

"Yep," Chandler replied. "But remember, it's very sharp and not to be used as a toy. You have to be very careful with it."

"Okay," the boy promised as he put the knife in his pocket.

Something in the sky caught Chandler's eye. He pointed his finger up at the dark object and said, "Hey, look! Up there."

Far above, a large eagle circled the treetops, looking to scoop up a meal from the ground below.

"Wouldn't it be great to be an eagle?" he asked the boy. "They might not look it, but they are one of the most dangerous animals in the forest. Between their sharp talons and beak they can be quite the fighter. And any problems, they can just soar up in the sky away from everyone and everything. Did you know they have no natural predators? That means they don't have to worry about getting eaten by any other animals around here. At least the full-grown ones don't."

The boy followed his finger, watching the large bird coast in circles, floating on the wind without even flapping its wings. "I'd love to fly in the air. Just like Superman."

Chandler agreed with a smile. He couldn't think of the last time he felt this happy and at peace. It's hard to imagine how far he had come in just a few short days. The life Chandler once knew, in almost complete isolation from the world except for his mother, was gone. It was a life he could never return to, even if he wanted. Not that he ever would. He felt like a butterfly who just emerged from its chrysalis. The past few days with Dylan had been incredible. But no matter how close his bond with Dylan became, something was still missing from their relationship... and she was sleeping back at the cabin.

"Hey," he said to the boy. "Do you want to head back now? I think your mom should be waking up soon."

"Awww. Let's keep exploring. She'll be fine," the boy pleaded.

"How about this? We go get your mom and come back out here to see what else we can find. Don't you think this would be even more fun if she was here with us? You can even be the lead explorer."

The boy's face lit up at the thought of being the leader. "Okay, sure!" he said.

With that, the two turned around and headed back to the cabin to check on their matriarch.

Chapter Twenty-Five

SAMANTHA WATCHED FROM THE front seat of her car as the man who abducted her walked through the field toward the cabin. Her precious son followed closely behind, unaware of the atrocities his companion committed. With a smile on his face and a spring in his step, the boy looked like he'd been having a great time.

So close to freedom, she thought nothing could stop her from starting the car and driving away. The key sat snugly in the ignition, waiting to be turned. Chandler was still too far away to reach her in time, but she couldn't leave her son behind. By the time she returned with the police, they could be long gone. For now, she'd have to put any thoughts of escape on hold.

As she continued to sink lower in her seat, she knew it didn't matter if they spotted her. Either way, she would have to exit the car and rejoin them. She thought about the mistakes she had made in life and considered if she was to blame for this entire situation. She certainly would do a lot of things differently if she had a do-over. Everyone makes mistakes, some bigger than others, and maybe in a way she deserved her fate, but it wasn't fair for Dylan to be stuck in the middle. It seemed Chandler made the boy happy, but she'd never be able to trust him with her child after the things he'd done. The fact that she was even sitting here debating it with herself was reason enough to get her head examined.

Instead of judging Chandler's child-rearing capability, she needed to think of a reason why she went out to the car. Even with willful ignorance on Chandler's part, he would have a hard time believing she went to the vehicle for any other reason than to flee. Hopefully Chandler would take pity on her. The thought of being tied up again made her quiver. She couldn't let that happen. Wishing she'd grabbed something to use as a weapon from the house when she had the chance, Samantha scanned the interior of her vehicle. All she found was a discarded juice box and a few small plastic toys in the backseat. Nothing that could help her in a fight.

As they approached the cabin, Chandler gave a few long glances toward the car. He must have spotted her. Expecting him to change his direction and come for her, she was surprised when he didn't miss a step and followed Dylan into the cabin. He knew she wouldn't leave without the boy.

Out of time and with nothing to defend herself, she opened the glove compartment in a last ditch effort to find something useful. She allowed the pile of papers and booklets to spill out onto the floor. Underneath the owner's manual, she spotted a medium-sized flashlight. Not the best weapon but better than going in empty-handed, even if it was just for peace of mind. She shoved the flashlight in her pocket and exited the car, making her way to the cabin to be reunited with her son.

Samantha opened the door and walked inside to see Chandler pouring Dylan a can of lemonade. The two were laughing, in the middle of a conversation about their favorite type of insect. If she didn't know better, it seemed like it was a scene from a picture perfect father/son bonding moment.

When the boy noticed her enter, he ran to her shouting, "Mom! Mom! C'mon. You have to check out what we found in the woods, and look what I got!" He pulled the closed pocket knife from his pants and held it out, proudly showing off his new folding blade.

She bent down to embrace the boy and said, "Hey, settle down. I've missed you. Are you okay?" Holding Dylan in her arms, she thought he felt bigger than the last time she saw him. It seemed like they'd been apart for months. The drugs had warped her sense of time, stretching the minutes and hours until they lost all meaning. Even though it had been less than two days since Chandler first entered her home, she could barely remember a life before this hell she had been forced into.

"What is this?" she asked, looking at the knife and furrowing her face.

"It's my pocket knife. It's important for all scouts to be prepared in the wilderness. I know it's not a toy. I'll be careful with it," the boy replied excitedly.

Samantha didn't approve of Dylan's new blade. Being only five years old, he was hardly responsible enough to be trusted with it. In any other situation, she would have taken it from him on the spot, but she had more important matters to deal with and she considered the possibility that the knife could be their ticket to freedom.

Finally, the adult's eyes met, each unsure how the other would react to their presence. When she saw the concern on Chandler's face, she felt she could use it as a weakness and returned a fierce gaze filled with false bravado. Seeing her son motivated her to put Chandler in his place and take Dylan home where they belonged.

"Why are you doing this?" she asked.

"Well, I thought some family bonding time would be good for us. I know this has been a rough few days for you and I'm sorry but..."

"A rough few days?" she said, cutting him off. "You broke into my house. You held me captive, and god only knows what else you did. Then you kidnapped me and my son and brought us to the middle of nowhere!"

"Calm down. I think you're exaggerating a few things. I would never hurt you or kidnap you," he replied, genuinely upset at the accusation.

"So I'm free to take Dylan and go home right now?" she asked.

The request caught Chandler off-guard. He stumbled over his words, unsure how to respond. He didn't want to hold her against her will, but he didn't want her to leave either. He just needed a little more time to prove that he could be the man of her dreams.

Dylan came to his rescue, breaking the silence. "Mom, what are you talking about? We just got here! Come with us to check out this trail in the woods. We found a river!" he said.

"Dylan, not now," she replied, dismissing the boy. Now that she finally had the wherewithal to confront Chandler, she was determined to make him see the madness of his actions.

"But Mom! We only came back to get you and bring you with us," the boy implored.

"I'm not going anywhere except home!" she yelled, frightening the child and causing him to cease his pleas and back away into the corner.

Chandler looked at the boy and understood his frustration. He wanted to forget this argument and go on a family hike as well. "Just give us a few minutes, okay pal?" he said and turned his attention back to Samantha. "Listen, I know you're under a lot of stress, but I thought we made some great progress yesterday. I just want what's best for us. There's no need to jump down each other's throats."

"I don't know what you think this is, but you're living in a fantasy! I'm not your wife! I'm already married." Her mind went to Kevin, realizing he was probably dead. Divorce was one thing, but she was too young to be a widow. "Did you kill Kevin?"

Chandler seethed at the mention of her previous husband. He had pushed the man and his untimely demise out of his conscious mind before inserting himself into the newly vacated role. The mere mention of the man's name chipped away at the facade, bringing him back to his old persona. Defensively, he replied, "He was no husband to you. I saw the way he treated you. The way he treated Dylan. You deserved better than that. You should be thanking me!"

Samantha laughed at the absurdity with tears streaming down her cheeks.

Chandler continued to plead his case, "I would never have treated you that way. You have to admit our time together was special. If you gave me a chance..."

"I'm sorry, okay!" she screamed, cutting him off, her voice cracking through the yell. "I made a mistake! We had been trying to get pregnant for a while and I was so frustrated. Kevin refused to see a fertility doctor and I felt so alone. He was working a late shift, and I saw you in the backyard. I was desperate and figured I would try something outside the box. Kevin never needed to know. But he knew. He knew right away because, apparently, he never wanted kids. He just didn't have the balls to tell me. So he went behind my back and had a vasectomy. A fucking vasectomy! The whole time we were trying to get pregnant and he saw how much pain it caused me. Meanwhile, he lied to me the entire time. That's why he never treated Dylan like a true son, and because he knew the truth. I deserved whatever punishment he gave me."

Chandler's mind reeled at the information overload. Deep down he knew Dylan was his son, but he could never face the elephant in the room and admit the truth, even to himself. His fractured mind felt like his brain was being pulled in two directions at the same time. On one side he was Kevin Reed and this was his family, but on the other he was the weird neighbor and just a stranger to these people.

Instead of including Chandler in the child's life, Kevin's rage at his wife's indiscretions caused him to forbid any contact between the boy and his true father. How could Chandler's already fragile mental state hold up under such circumstances? He had been forced to live next door and watch his son grow up without ever getting to know him. It was enough to drive anyone to the brink of sanity.

Chandler clenched his eyes shut, pressing his palms against his temples, trying to stop the debilitating headache. His grip on reality had eroded to the point where he could no longer differentiate truth from fantasy. He felt like his head would explode at any moment, and a part of him wished it did. Things would be easier that way.

Samantha noticed his distracted mental state and looked around the room for something to attack him with. This might be her only opening. She wondered if she could make it to the kitchen for a knife without alerting Chandler. After she made her move, she would only get one chance to kill him before he overpowered her.

She took one tentative step, keeping her eyes on Chandler. He made no move toward her. On her second step, she glanced around the room and couldn't shake the feeling that something was missing.

“Dylan?” she said quietly. With no reply, she repeated her son’s name again, louder this time. There weren’t many places to hide in the small cabin. A bout of panic erupted inside of her. The boy was gone.

Chapter Twenty-Six

CHANDLER AND SAMANTHA RACED out of the cabin, both of them calling Dylan's name at the top of their lungs. Samantha's thoughts of sneaking into the kitchen for a knife became just a fractured piece of a plan that would never come to fruition. Frantically, she scanned the area for her son. She looked in the backyard and towards the tree line surrounding the cabin but saw no sign of him. Slipping away during their argument, she didn't know how long he had been missing. He could be anywhere by now.

"This way," said Chandler, running toward the same path he had taken with the boy earlier.

Samantha followed him, continuing to scan the woods as she went, looking for any signs of her son. Her panic rising with every step, she called for Dylan at regular intervals on their journey, but her heart sank each time she yelled and heard nothing in return.

While only a few moments ago she thought of killing Chandler or escaping at all costs, now she desperately needed his help to find her son. A genuine look of concern on his face both scared and calmed her at the same time. The boy could have gone in any direction, but Chandler seemed sure of the boy's path. Having explored the area with Dylan earlier, she saw no reason to argue with him.

Traveling through the woods as quickly as they could manage, they arrived at the stream where Chandler and Dylan stopped earlier in less than half the time of the boys' original trek. With no trace of the child in sight, Chandler came to a stop at the edge and looked down the waterway in each direction.

"Why are we stopping?" Samantha asked impatiently. She knew that with every wasted second, the boy could be getting further and further away from them.

Chandler put his finger to his lips, indicating for her to remain silent. He strained his ears to pick up any sounds that could lead them to Dylan, but between the running water and the rustling of leaves in the wind, he was at a loss. The trip was not going the way he envisioned.

Suddenly, he yelled at the top of his lungs, startling Samantha with the outburst. "Dylan! Dylan!"

Only the chirping birds in the distance answered his call. He was certain the boy would have come this way, but if he went further it could be in any direction. He took a moment to scan the area for footprints, but the long grass covered any tracks the boy would have made.

"This is as far as I came with him earlier. We talked about exploring further but came back for you first."

Samantha already felt responsible for Dylan's disappearance, and Chandler's words only exacerbated her thoughts of blame. The boy was old enough to know not to run off in the woods alone, but with the adults arguing, she couldn't blame him for wanting to escape. Even though Samantha considered Chandler a lunatic, the man had won over the boy's affection easily. But now, with the child's life in peril, her fears of Chandler fled. He was her best hope of finding Dylan.

Then Chandler remembered something he said to the boy. "I told him if he's lost in the woods and he finds a stream, he should follow the flow and it will lead towards civilization. So maybe he followed the water downhill," he said, pointing downstream. He felt like he was grasping at straws with the suggestion, but it was the only idea could think of.

"No," replied Samantha. "Not towards civilization, away from it. With us yelling, he would want to be alone. So he would have gone that way." She pointed in the other direction, leading deeper into the forest.

"Okay, if that's what you think," said Chandler, conceding to mother's intuition.

"Maybe we should split up?" Samantha suggested.

"No, that's not a good idea. The last thing we need is for you to get lost out here as well." After a moment to consider their options, he added, "How about this? We'll check up this way and if we don't find him, I'll bring you back to the cabin and you can wait there in case he shows back up on his own while I go back out and look some more."

"Okay, good idea," Samantha said. She hadn't even considered the fact he might return to the cabin.

The pair headed along the stream's edge, going against the current while they continued to alternate between calling for the lost boy and listening for any clues as to his whereabouts.

After another ten minutes of walking with no luck in finding Dylan, they were both losing hope that the boy had traveled this way. With their quick pace, they should have run into him by now if they were on the same path. Searching the woods for the lost child was not how either of them expected their day to go. Samantha's concern for her son overtook any feelings of fear or anger she had at the man who brought her here. For Chandler, the search seemed to be the perfect experience to bring the two adults closer together and build trust between them. He wished he was a little better at carrying on a conversation, but just being with her and working toward a common goal was good enough for now. Even though he felt good about their budding relationship, he knew that if they didn't find the boy soon, things would turn sour quickly.

Chandler broke the silence, saying aloud what Samantha had already been thinking. "I don't think he came this way. We should have found him by now. Let's turn back here."

Samantha's heart sank realizing Chandler shared the same thought. With little other choice, the pair turned around and headed back before they wasted too much of the day looking in the wrong direction.

Chapter Twenty-Seven

OFFICER LUIS PEREZ SAT at his desk in the park ranger station finishing up his morning coffee, when he noticed it. Looking through the window of the outpost, he spotted a thin trail of smoke rising from the trees in the distance. There were a few cabins in that direction, but as far as he knew, they should all be empty at this time of year. Hunting season didn't open for a few months, and until that time, the area was usually a ghost town.

He grumbled to himself about the annoyance. During the quiet season, he had become accustomed to lounging around the office watching daytime television for most of his shift, maybe catching up on a little paperwork. On a lucky day, he might even sneak in a quick afternoon nap. Unfortunately for Luis, this would not be one of those days.

He wondered if a group of kids got into a cabin for a night of drinking. It wouldn't be the first time he had to evict a bunch of hungover teenagers from a night of partying. With the recent budget cuts, the station went unmanned at night this time of year, and they could have easily slipped in undetected. He had half a mind to ignore it and let them have their fun but if they started a forest fire, it would be his ass. The ranger took his time drinking his coffee while he finished the morning talk show on the television before putting on his jacket and getting ready to head over to break up the party. He left the comfort of the outpost and started up the station's ATV. Before speeding off to check out the disturbance, he mumbled a brief prayer hoping to make it back to the station before lunch.

He followed the trail of smoke up the dirt road, which led Luis directly to the dilapidated cabin. He pulled up to the green Subaru Outback and parked his ATV alongside it. Upon seeing the lone car, he breathed a little easier. With only one car parked in the driveway, maybe it was just some horny lovebirds looking for a little alone time rather than a drunken house party. Kicking out an embarrassed couple always proved easier than a group of drunks. Either way, Luis just wanted to get this over with.

He hopped off the ATV and headed towards the front door, giving it a hefty knock with his fist. The strike caused the unlatched door to creek open, allowing the ranger an opportunity to pop his head inside. Officer Perez loudly announced his presence but heard nothing in reply. After a moment, he entered the abandoned building, inspecting the cabin for any signs of trespass. Almost immediately, he spotted personal belongings in the bedroom and an empty suitcase on the floor but saw no sign of their owners. Checking out the fireplace, the source of the smoke that brought him there, he confirmed the smoldering embers posed no threat to the structure. Deeming it to be under control, he headed back outside to look around for the troublemakers.

Taking a loop around the building, Luis didn't see a trace of anyone in the immediate vicinity. Since there didn't seem to be any imminent danger and he didn't feel like waiting around all day for the squatters to return, he figured his best course of action would be to head back to the station for now. He could come back to check on the cabin in a few hours–after he ate the lunch his fiancé packed him this morning. She made the best sandwiches. His thoughts kept circling back to the food waiting patiently to be eaten back in the office refrigerator.

Just as he was about to hop on his ATV and take off, he decided he might as well take one quick precaution before heading out. Picking up his radio, he called down to the local police station. "Hey, this is Officer Perez at the park ranger station. Can you run a license plate check for me? I found a car parked out here at an empty cabin with no operator. It's a green Subaru Outback, New York plate number Kilo Alpha Echo 2357."

The speaker crackled before a voice came through. "Sure thing buddy, give me a minute and I'll pull it up. How's everything going out there? You ready to apply for a position on the force and start working with the big boys?"

Luis replied, laughing, "Hey, I like it at the ranger center. It's nice and quiet over here. I don't have to deal with half of the bullshit that gets flung at you guys every day."

"Yeah, well... to each his own. I'll get back to you in a minute with that plate lookup."

Not overly concerned with the results of the check, he jumped back on the ATV and started up the engine. He put the vehicle in reverse, ready to hightail it back to the station. Just before backing out of the driveway, he took one last glance at the car next to him. What he saw inside the car startled him into doing a double take. He blinked his eyes repeatedly to confirm his sight.

How did he miss this when he first pulled up? The annoyance of being dragged out here in the first place must have distracted him. Lying in the back seat of the Subaru, fast asleep, was a young child.

Chapter Twenty-Eight

WHEN SAMANTHA AND CHANDLER emerged from the tree line, both of their hearts jumped at the surprising sight in front of them. They immediately spotted the officer standing with Dylan by the car. The ranger's quad idled unattended while he questioned the boy. Samantha's only thought remained with her son. An instant feeling of relief washed over her, knowing that he was safe. She didn't even consider the man talking with Dylan and what he could mean for their rescue.

In contrast to Samantha focusing on her child, Chandler's attention remained fixated on the officer encroaching on his hideaway. It was another interruption to their family bonding time. Clenching his teeth, along with his fists, he seethed at the disturbance. Incredulous at the lack of respect for his privacy, he knew this was going to be a problem. He checked his pockets, already knowing they were empty. In his haste to look for the missing boy, he left his police-issued gun behind. Considering it unlikely to talk his way out of this one, he'd have to find another way to eliminate this new threat to his family. He looked at Samantha and sighed.

Why did he keep getting into these situations with her around? He hoped she wasn't bringing him bad luck. God only knows what this would do to their relationship. He'd never felt closer to her than on their search for Dylan, except maybe in the shower the previous day, and he didn't want anything to disrupt their budding connection.

Upon seeing her lost child, Samantha broke out into a run towards the boy, shouting his name as she went. Chandler kept pace with her, concerned only with the ranger's response to their approach.

In the ten minutes since finding the boy, Officer Perez heard back from the station about his license plate request. Apparently, police had been searching for a missing elderly woman when they stumbled upon numerous bodies in two adjacent houses. The tag came back as belonging to a resident of the house where they found the deceased elderly woman. Although currently unknown how the driver was involved in the killings, the station warned Luis to be on high alert.

Officer Perez awoke the child and immediately peppered him with questions. "Who are you? What are you doing here? Where are your parents?" But having just been awoken from a nap, the boy remained obstinate, refusing to speak with the officer. The ranger had successfully coaxed the child out of the car only a minute before he spotted the two adults coming toward him from the woods.

As they approached, Luis raised his firearm, pointing it at the pair. "Stop where you are. Don't move any closer. Identify yourself."

Noticing the officer's threatening gesture toward his mother, Dylan yelled, "Mom!"

The two slowed their run but still advanced towards the officer with their hands raised in a show of harmlessness.

"Hold on a minute. Put the gun down," Chandler said, hoping to diffuse the situation.

Undeterred, Luis held the gun steady at the pair. "What are you folks doing here?" he asked.

This was Samantha's chance to tell the officer everything. She could warn him of the atrocities committed by the psychopath who kidnapped her. He could arrest the man and end this nightmare once and for all.

Just as she built up the courage to call out her abductor, Chandler spoke. "Sorry to worry you officer, we were just on a family getaway. My uncle used to take me to this cabin when I was a boy."

Luis kept the gun trained on Chandler. "I'm not stupid," he said. "I called in the plate number on that car. I don't know what you've been up to, but I think they'd like to ask both of you some questions down at the station... and before you go getting any funny ideas, backup is already on the way, should be here any minute."

Chandler considered his options, but he didn't see a way out of this. He felt a panic attack setting in. It couldn't end like this. He stood only a few paces away from the man but with the gun pointed directly at him, he'd never get to him in time. The situation had spiraled out of control. He glanced at Samantha and knew she would be no help. Half of him expected her to make a break for the officer, screaming for the ranger to shoot him. Staring at the weapon, she had the look of a deer frozen in headlights, unsure of which direction to run.

Remaining still and doing nothing was out of the question as well. He couldn't go to jail. He'd rather let the officer shoot him here and die in this spot than be locked up in a cell. The thought of being stuck in a cage and studied by doctors the rest of his life, never allowed to see his family again–no, he couldn't allow that.

He felt his body tense up as he got ready to spring forward in a last ditch attempt, but just as he was about to jump, the officer let out a blood-curdling scream. In one motion, the ranger fell to his knee and slammed the butt of his gun down into Dylan's head, knocking the boy to the ground.

Samantha screamed for her boy. "Dylan!"

Sticking from Luis's thigh, pushed in all the way to the hilt, was Dylan's pocket knife. A thin trickle of blood rolled down his pants from the wound. Noticing Chandler's panicked state, and with the gun trained on both of the people he cared most about, the boy took matters into his own hands.

The next few seconds seemed to move in both slow motion and fast forward at the same time. Seeing her injured son fall to the floor from the officer's crushing blow, Samantha lunged forward toward her son to prevent any more harm from coming to him. Inspecting his injured leg, the officer saw Samantha's movement from the corner of his eye. Instinctively, Officer Perez looked up and pulled the trigger. A loud bang echoed through the trees, disturbing the peaceful forest and sending the birds scattering from their perches.

Samantha looked like a cartoon character, hovering stationary in the air for a moment before falling to the ground with a thud. The bullet lodged in her chest seemed to halt the forward momentum of her jump and brought her crashing to the ground in a cloud of dust. Unsure what had happened, she felt a tightness in her chest when she tried to breathe. She inhaled and felt an immediate pain in her lung. Laying flat on her stomach only exacerbated her struggle for air.

Officer Perez's jaw hung open in surprise. Lowering his weapon, he stared at the woman in disbelief of his own actions. He'd never shot a person before. Kneeling, paralyzed, almost in as much shock as Samantha herself, the ranger wondered if he made a mistake pulling the trigger. In the moment, he didn't even have time to think. The last thing he wanted to deal with was an internal affairs investigation and the never ending pile of paperwork this would bring.

Gazing at the mortally injured woman and considering how this would affect his career, he remained fixed on his thoughts for a moment too long. Wondering if she would survive, Luis took no notice of Chandler's final approach until the man's hands had already closed around his neck. Startled out of his daze by the sudden attack, Luis tried to swing the gun around, but Chandler was already on top of him. With the officer still kneeling on his injured leg, Chandler pushed the ranger to the ground, pinning his back while he increased the pressure on the man's windpipe.

With his gun hand pushed tightly against his chest by the force of Chandler's weight, Luis flailed his other arm wildly as he struggled to breathe. Balling up his fist, he punched Chandler in the back, beating him repeatedly with his free hand, but the force on his neck only increased with each punch.

In a last ditch effort, Officer Perez thrashed his free hand desperately until it came upon Dylan's knife, still sticking in his leg. In his state of panic, he'd forgotten the injury until his hand found the weapon's handle. He pulled the blade from his leg, causing a burning hot bolt of pain to shoot all the way up his spine. Trying his best to ignore the excruciating pain, he plunged the knife into Chandler's flank, causing the man to grunt in surprise. Finally, the grip on his neck loosened. Luis took the small window of opportunity to inhale, giving some relief to his oxygen-starved lungs. He pulled the knife from Chandler's side and prepared to strike again.

Dylan watched the scuffle play out in front of him, and although he wanted to go tend to his mother, he knew Chandler needed help. With time running out, he took hold of the ranger's wrist and used the only weapon he had left. Opening his mouth wide, Dylan clamped his jaw down on the officer's hand, sinking his teeth into the man's flesh. The metallic taste of blood filled Dylan's mouth, but he kept his jaw clenched tight around the man's skin, fighting the instinct to recoil at the acrid flavor.

Luis would have screamed in pain if he had any air left to expel. The knife fell to the ground as the boy continued to tear at the meaty tissue between the officer's thumb and index finger like a wild dog.

With his only weapon lost and hopes of survival rapidly fading, Officer Luis Perez thought of his fiancé and all the years they wouldn't get to spend together. The lack of oxygen to his brain had already started affecting his memory. As his light faded out, he spent his final moment unsuccessfully trying to remember his lovely bride-to-be's name.

Chandler continued to squeeze the ranger's throat until long after the man had expired. He snapped out of the position only after a weak cough from behind broke him out of the stupor. Letting go of the dead man's neck, he turned and rushed to Samantha's aid.

Chandler gently rolled Samantha onto her back, relieving the pressure on her chest. She coughed again, louder this time, and a plume of red mist sprayed from her mouth. The dark purple spot on her shirt grew as blood pumped from her wound. The growing stain rapidly spread across her chest as she lay on her back in shock. She looked from Dylan to Chandler, and even though her glossed over eyes couldn't focus on their faces, she knew they were there with her. She opened her mouth to speak, but a sharp pain in her chest prevented the words from escaping her lungs. Her mouth felt dry even as she continued to cough up more blood, coating her lips in a bright red sheen. She looked as if a toddler had gotten into their mother's makeup and applied a thick layer of lipstick.

With the last of her energy and at great effort, she whispered. "Take care of Dylan. I'm sorry." Her head rolled to the side as she exhaled her final breath.

Chandler didn't even have time to process Samantha's death when the faint sound of a siren in the distance reminded him they had to go before more trouble arrived. He bent down and ran his fingers through Samantha's hair one last time, kissing her softly on the lips before standing back up and walking towards the car. He opened the trunk and retrieved the camping backpack he prepared and a second, smaller bag filled with food. The boy remained on the ground next to his dead mother, hugging her lifeless body and crying.

"I hate to do this, but we have to go," he said to the child. "More bad men are on the way."

Dylan looked up at him. "Okay," he said as he stood and wiped his tears. In place of the tears, he smeared his face with his mother's blood that soaked through his sleeve during their embrace.

The boy took one last look at his mom and turned to follow Chandler, who had already begun walking towards the woods. Instead of taking the same, well-worn path they hiked on earlier, Chandler led them a less traveled route, one in which they would hopefully have a long head start before anyone knew to look for them.

When he caught up with his new guardian, Dylan noticed him holding his side where he had been stabbed. “Are you okay?” he asked the man, worried for his only companion.

“Yeah, I’ll be fine. We’ll stop to bandage it up in a bit. I guess it’s just gonna be me and you now, buddy.”

“That’s alright,” said the boy before asking, “Can I call you Dad from now on?”

Chandler smiled at the request. “I’d like that, son. I’d like that a lot.” He ruffled Dylan’s hair as they disappeared into the trees, embarking on the biggest adventure of their lives.

Acknowledgements

A few people I wanted to thank for their support:

The first thanks goes to my editor Heather Ann Larson, for going through the manuscript more times than I can count to fix all of my misplaced commas and my beta readers Derek Thomas & Samantha Hawkins.

Special thanks to everyone who read and reviewed my first book. There's too many to list but a few that really shouted about it: Tasha Schiedel, Corrina Morse, Samantha Hawkins (2nd mention!), Linda Milito Martin, Rhonda Lynn Bobbitt, Leigh Kenny, Melissa Coffman, Theresa Hayden, Emily Keenan, and Bill Gilbert.

The entire indie horror community for being so supportive of each other.

My daughter Lyla who has her own ideas for a book. My son Jacob, who is jumping on my head mid sentence less these days (he usually asks before attacking me now) and of course my wife Amellia for letting me continue on the escapade.

Anyone who made it this far putting up with twisted thoughts.

Also By LM Kaplin

Fang Fiction: Vampire Horror Stories

This collection of short stories will take you on an emotional rollercoaster through time with ten dark tales of fangs and flesh. You'll follow the evolution of the vampire species beginning with the original vampire circa 1000 BC and ending in a dystopian future with humans on the verge of extinction.

About the Author

LM Kaplin lives in upstate New York and has been a horror enthusiast in all forms his entire life. His morbid obsession with the macabre started one night while watching Poltergeist as a young child. The next morning, he began searching for ancient burial grounds in the backyard. Dismayed at not uncovering any evil spirits, he buried his own demons for future generations to find. It's time to start digging them up.

Find him on Facebook or Instagram or email him at LMKaplin@gmail.com

If you enjoyed this book, please consider leaving a review on Amazon, GoodReads, or your favorite social media platform.

www.ingramcontent.com/pod-product-compliance
Ingram Content Group UK Ltd.
Pitfield, Milton Keynes, MK11 3LW, UK
UKHW041954190726
13854UKWH00005B/1971